THE EIGHTH HUSBAND

MAY HOWELL BEECHER

Published by Left of Brain Books

Copyright © 2021 Left of Brain Books

ISBN 978-1-396-31895-5

First Edition

Table of Contents

"The angel said to the young man, Brother, today we shall lodge with Raguel who is thy cousin; he hath also one only daughter named Sara; I will speak for her that she may be given thee for a wife.

"Then the young man answered the angel, I have heard, brother Azarius, that the maid hath been given to seven men who all died in the marriage chamber."

Apocrypha—Tobit,
Chapter 6: 10-13

CHAPTER I

THE CURSE

It was the fifth day of May in the year of our Lord 1817. All the early morning the weather had been threatening. At the noon hour the rain fell in torrents and the lowland meadows were soon transformed into ponds. At sunset the clouds parted and a rift of golden splendor illumined the west, dying away in crimson glory beyond the green verdure of the hills.

A young and comely woman stood leaning against the stile that did duty as gateway to the old farmhouse. Shading her eyes with her hand, she gazed along the roadway that led to the town. She had been alone all day, for it was training day and all the men folks were enjoying a holiday. Raguel, her husband, was an officer of the state militia and had gone away in the early morning, well pleased that his little wife should see him in his gay regimentals.

Only two weeks had elapsed since he had brought Edna, his girl-bride, to dwell in the old farmhouse at the foot of the mountain.

As she scanned the road, instead of the loved form of her young husband, she saw a bent, strange looking figure, leaning on a staff, slowly advancing over the hill. Stray locks of gray hair hung over the scarred, uncanny looking face that was framed by a faded red hood.

Edna's heart beat fast, almost to suffocation, for she was a timid little body, and the strange appearing creature would have caused anxiety, if not alarm, to one of a less nervous temperament. She hastily retraced her footsteps towards the house, entering and closing the door, knowing that she had been seen and that in all probability the woman would enter the house, for there was nothing to hinder her from so doing if she desired. There was no lock on the door or other mode of fastening except the latch, for Raguel held to the rule that had governed his ancestors, that the latchstring must always be hanging out in hospitable greeting to all who desired entertainment, and in the house she waited In fear and trembling.

Up the winding pathway, where the cinnamon roses were putting forth their green leaves, hobbled the bent figure of the old woman. As she reached the house, instead of sounding the old brass knocker on the door, she brought the large knob of the heavy staff that she carried down against the panels with a loud, resounding thud. Edna, with trembling hands, opened the door and stepped far back in the wide entry. The elflike creature made a low, mocking bow, then spread out her scant skirts in a curtsey, as if to emphasize her pretended reverence, as she slowly straightened up, making a great effort to stand erect, which was a physical impossibility. She said:

"You are a fine looking wench, but at your age I was much handsomer, and I never wasted my time watching and waiting for a recreant knight. A woman and a dog will chase after a gay uniform, even if it leads them to the devil and he who wears regimentals wears also a thick coating of conceit plastered on by the silly maids and matrons who bow down and worship the brass buttons the fools wear for their adornment."

And turning her eyes upward, she chanted:

"Your feasts shall be turned into mourning, and all your mirth into lamentations.

"Don't look so frightened, simpleton. I'll not harm a hair of your head, but there's a many who will not prove so kind. A curse hangs over your head by a silken thread, taut at the present time, but before many moons have come and gone the silken thread shall weaken, the strands shall slip apart, and the curse will fall.

"Only one child—a girl—shall gladden your heart, and she might better remain unborn than to suffer all that fate holds in store for her ere the gates of heaven open to receive. Though blameless, yet shall she be accursed. I have spoken."

Ere the last wards died away Edna had fallen on the hard floor, a limp, unconscious form.

The old woman spurned her with her foot, saying:

"Poor, weak fool! And it is such as she that strong men love. But the eagle may not mate with the dove, and the curse shall fall." And without another glance at the prostrate form, she adjusted her old red hood, and wrapping the faded blue cloth mantle about her bent shoulders, she wended her way down the wooded path to the highway.

Raguel, coming home from a mimic war, saw the wrinkled face and the glare of malice in the woman's eyes as she passed him in the road, and wondered greatly; then in sudden fear lightly touched the whip to the black horse that carried him so proudly, remembering that Edna was alone and doubtless had been frightened if the woman had stopped at the farmhouse, for her appearance was that of a wild creature.

He could not recall ever having seen the woman about the neighborhood. If his father were living—and so desired—he could have told him the woman's history. A poor half-breed Indian, educated above her station by a white father, she had given her foolish trusting heart, as her mother had done before her, to a white man (a wasted love and a ruined life) the gay ship's captain, who had sailed away after making shipwreck of her happiness. The man returned after a few years from foreign parts with his pretty girl-wife, to settle down in the old homestead at the foot of the mountains, giving no thought to the poor creature at the town poorhouse who was a mental wreck with lucid intervals when half-formed plans for revenge entered her crazy head. She would disappear for weeks at a time; no one knew how she lived or where she wandered to during these intervals. Then she would put in an appearance again to be cared for at the poorhouse.

Raguel rode swiftly on his way to the farmhouse and, quickly alighting from the saddle, entered the house. Edna's unconscious form was in the entryway, and to the horrified young husband the cold, white face looked like death. As he gathered her close in his arms there was a faint movement of the eyelids, and with a startled expression her eyes looked up at him. With glad recognition she exclaimed:

"Oh, Raguel, I am so glad that you are here. I have been so frightend. A horrible old woman came here and said such awful things to me. Where has she gone?"

Starting up in affright, she asked, "Did you see her?"

"Yes, I met her down the road," said Raguel. "I think she must be crazy, judging from her looks, and not responsible for anything that she said. Try not to mind it; don't think of it again, dear. She cannot harm you."

To the nervous, hysterical woman it was not easy to forget or refrain from speaking the fears that the old woman's words had suggested to her mind.

One of the neighbors came in next day, and Edna told her the story in all its details. The woman had heard all about the crazy woman years before, and without daring to say outright all that she knew, she managed to convey to

Edna's mind that something was being kept back, a mystery that concerned her to know.

Still troubled in thought, Edna that evening asked Raguel if he knew what Mrs. Payson meant, and if there was any secret connecting them with the old Indian woman, adding:

"She made me so uncomfortable by her innuendoes, but I would not please her by inquiring what she meant, because I knew she was just dying to tell me."

"Of course she was, and what does it all amount to—just crazy talk. I wish that woman would mind her own business and keep away from here. It is just as Otto" (the farm hand) "says, 'She talks so much and she says noddings.'"

"I know," said Edna. "She came in the other day as I held a small mirror in my hand, and she said, 'Law sakes, I guess you must think yourself handsome.' 'Yes,' said I, 'I do.' Then she tossed her head and asked, 'What made you have a turned up nose?' And I answered, 'So that it would not always be poking itself into other folks' business.' You know that she has an awful long nose. She looked mad, but she did not say any more."

"Ha, ha! I am glad if you can hold your own with her, and that was a pretty good shot. All the same, I wish she would keep away from here. Association with her is not good for you, and the hateful things she is so fond of saying rankle."

CHAPTER II

The Birth of a Child

The weeks and months passed on until the May training day was at hand again. The purple and white lilacs were putting forth their fragrant blossoms, and over hill and dale the grass looked like great squares of green velvet.

In the front room at the homestead, not far from the fireplace, a large, old-fashioned wooden cradle stood; handed down for several generations, it had been the first resting place of the little new comers to the old house. With pillows of softest down, and white quilted blankets, it was ready for another occupant. Folded away in sweet lavender blossoms were tiny garments of softest linen, spun and woven by the little mistress of the house, who was looking forward to the time when a baby face with Raguel's blue eyes should look up to her in all the beauty of infantile innocence. Many times Edna would say:

"If the child is a boy I shall be content, for then I shall know that all of the old woman's talk was nonesense, but if it is a girl child I shall have great fears."

Raguel had tried to calm her anxiety, for her condition was giving him grave concern. She would waken in the night trembling with fear, and to Raguel's questioning made answer that every night a woman in a white gown came down from the attic and stood at the foot of the bed, brandishing a large knife. She would vanish when Edna screamed in her agony of fear. A nervous chill would follow the harassing scene, and it would be nearly daylight before she fell into a troubled slumber. All this was telling on her strength, which was not great at any time.

One morning, after an unusually distressing night, she was so ill that they sent for the doctor. Doctor Munson was a kind-hearted, sensible old gentleman. After gaining Edna's confidence he questioned her about the apparition, and asked to examine the door that opened from her sleeping room on the attic stairs. There was no lock on the door. The doctor suggested putting a bolt on above the latch, so that it could be securely fastened. The ruse was successful, and the woman in white never put in an appearance again.

One dark night, while a heavy thunderstorm was raging, Edna was taken sick. Doctor Munson was hastily summoned. All night and the day following he was in constant attendance. The day was dark and gloomy, the rain still falling in torrents. To the anxious watchers a great fear had come, for death hovered near and might at any moment bring desolation to the household. Just as the sun went down in a black cloud beyond the western hill an infant's cry was heard in the old house. The young mother heard it and rallied from her half-unconscious state to inquire:

"Is it a boy?"

The doctor raised his hand in admonition to the nurse, and replied:

"Yes, dear, it is all right."

A smile of glad content illuminated the wan face, and with a restful sigh her head settled back on the pillow.

The little one was a girl with wonderful, blue eyes that held within their depths a look of patient resignation.

The nurse said:

"She is the oldest looking baby at birth that I ever set eyes on. She looks as if she might be three months old this minute, and that air strange, far-off look in her eyes gives me the fidgets. I hope that she's going to live, but I dunno. She don't look as if she were long for this world. And how we'll ever tell Mis' Raguel the truth about her is more than I know or can guess. I shift all the responsibility on the doctor's shoulders. It's his mess, not mine, and he's got to git out of it the best way he can. Though I do suppose the poor creeter would ha' died if he hadn't deceived her."

The young mother came slowly back to health and strength, and at last to a knowledge of the little one's sex. The doctor told her the truth in the gentlest manner possible. The shock was so great that only the immediate use of restoratives prevented her from losing consciousness. The doctor felt that it was necessary for the matter to be straightened out at once. The crazy woman's words had made a deep impression on Edna's mind, weakened by her illness. The doctor told her that if the truth had not been withheld from her at the critical period of her sickness the result might have been fatal, and with calm, gentle words he tried to convince her of the folly of placing any credence on the foolish wanderings of an insane person.

Then he placed the beautiful little girl in her arms. Baby commenced to cry and, with a hysterical sob, Edna clasped the little one to her breast. Mother-love and anxiety rose uppermost; she wiped away her own tears and hushed her babe to sleep. The doctor went on his way, feeling sure that each would comfort the other, and that time would set all things right.

They named the baby Sara, and she grew and thrived in spite of nurse's prediction to the contrary. Her pretty face and dainty ways were a revelation and source of great delight to her parents.

Mrs. Payson said (but not in Edna's presence, for she had been spoken to by Raguel in a very plain manner after Edna's illness, and warned that it would not be safe for her to say anything about the child that would tend to increase the mother's fears), "that it was her opinion that there child of Raguel's would raise the mischief with men's hearts, and she for one believed the crazy woman's words would come true, for even as a baby she seemed to bewitch menfolks, and it was sickening to hear some folks rave over her beauty, which would most likely be the ruin of her."

Sara developed early a great love for flowers, and would sit in her little chair for hours at a time in the garden, watching the flowers, the bees, and the butterflies. The winged visitors there were so accustomed to her presence that they would come and go as undisturbed as if she were a part of the garden. Just above her head the trumpet flowers were blooming, and Sara became friendly with a little hummingbird that always hovered there among the blossoms. The tiny bird would flutter about her curls and rest for a second on her hand without the slightest appearance of fear.

One day Tom, the house cat, came out to the garden for a frolic. He saw the humming bird just poising above the flowers, and with one bound he crashed among the vines, and then appeared with the little bird in his mouth.

Sara gave a startled scream and then grasped Mr. Tom by the throat, and quick as a flash the little captive was set free. Its beautiful plumage was ruffled and the bird seemed to be nearly dead, but Sara fixed up a little box for it in the house, and after a few hours it rallied and sipped the sweetened water prepared for it, and was soon winging its flight.

Edna had tried to instill in the little one's heart a love for and tenderness towards all of God's creatures, but Sara had her peculiarities.

She had a rag dolly, and dolly's dress was pinned together with tiny thorns. They were thrust through the cloth into dolly's body. One day it occurred to Sara that it was a cruel thing to do, and as she drew them out, her tears fell fast—she was deep in the pangs of remorse at what dolly must have suffered, pierced by the cruel thorns.

In a few minutes Sara was in the garden and had rolled away one of the large stones that rested against the stone wall. Out walked several daddy longlegs, and she remembered the thorns in her apron pocket. As the poor daddies scrambled along, she stuck a thorn in the body of each. That was like Sara—tender-hearted about some things, impulsive and incorrigible in many ways, yet always lovable and charming.

Her education commenced when she was three years old. She was started off to the district school, and soon became the pet of the older pupils, who never tired of repeating her smart sayings and pert ways.

In the winter the big boys stopped with their sleds to carry her to and from school, and her mother often had to settle the disputes arising among them, for each lad desired to be the chosen one. She reigned a little queen over many subjects. She was a lovely little maiden, small and slender, yet perfectly formed—a wonderful expression in the blue eyes that sometimes were almost black in their intensity.

When she was eight years old she was the promised wife of half a dozen boys, who considered themselves quite old enough to ask that momentous question at the mature age of ten years and were looking forward to the time when the promise should be fulfilled.

One boy made a confidant of his chum, and was informed:

"That's nothing; she's engaged to all the other fellers, too."

And when he chided her for her faithlessness, she cried and said that she thought he was real mean. She had said yes to the other boys because she did not want any fuss or bother. She just told them so for fun anyway, but she really intended to marry him, and after they were married the others could not help themselves and would have to be content with just being friends.

The boy appeared to be satisfied with the explanation, but would probably have had his doubts if he could have been a listener when she had her

confidential talks with the other boys. And yet her mother had taught her that one should always speak the truth, repeating the story of Ananias, whom God had punished by death because he told a lie.

"Dropped right down dead, did he?" Sara inquired. "Well, it may be true, but I cannot believe that God would kill any one just for telling lies. I should sooner think that it was a fit that made them die, just like old Mr. Grey had. He died that way, you know, and folks said he brought it on himself by drinking too much cider. I have known lots of folks who told lies, and they are all living." And that question settled to her own satisfaction, she went back to play with her rag dolly.

When she was twelve years old the hired man became desperately in love with her. He was a Scotchman, taciturn and sullen in disposition. Sara took delight in attracting his attention, and making him smile at her antics.

He had been called a woman hater, and was always saying sarcastic things about the sex. At first he looked at Sara in amazement, something after the manner of a large Newfoundland dog when a frisky kitten dances up to him. She seemed so innocent and guileless, with her little, coquettish airs and graces, that he gradually came under the glamour and was devoted to her, bringing the choicest fruit and prettiest flowers from off the hillside. After a time he would sit in moody silence, watching her flitting about the house, his eyes following her every movement.

Edna noticed his manner, and was displeased. She gave voice to her anxiety at last and told Raguel that she thought it would be best for him to send the man away.

Raguel ridiculed the idea, saying that it was absurd to think of the man having any feeling towards Sara excepting the natural admiration that all must feel towards a pretty child.

One day his eyes were opened. Cameron, the Scotchman, came to him and declared that Sara must be given to him in marriage. He said that he wanted her for a wife, and that he wanted to be married at once, without any delay. Raguel noted his wild manner and tried to reason with him. The man thrust a parcel of papers into Raguel's hands, saying:

"There is proof that I am of noble family. What more do you want?"

In the end it was necessary to hand him over to the authorities. From the townhouse where he was detained came reports of his ravings, always pleading with the keeper that Sara should be sent for. The man died a few weeks later, a raving maniac.

That was the beginning of serious attentions from all quarters, until Sara was admonished by her parents in this wise:

"Do not turn your eyes towards any man young or old; look down as a modest girl should when a man's eyes are on her."

"Yes," said Sara, "that would be smart. Then they will rave over my beautiful, long eyelashes, and the girls will say I do it just to show how pretty I look that way. How will I know they are looking at me unless I look at them? You had better put blinders on me and be done with it!" And she flounced out of the room.

Mrs. Eaton, one of the neighbors, died and Edna sent Sara to the house with her arms full of the early blossoms from the garden, for Mrs. Eaton had been very fond of flowers. The sweet apple tree was laden with bloom, and Edna remembered how her kind neighbor had once stopped beneath the tree when, as now, it was in full flower, and had said "apple blossoms, she thought, were the sweetest flowers on earth." So Edna broke off large bunches of the sweet, pink flowers and added them to the garlands in Sara's arms. And thus the young girl tripped across lots to the Eaton homestead, a sweet picture in an apple blossom frame.

She came back in a few minutes, her face bathed in tears, although the expression of her countennace betokened anger more than sorrow. In broken words she told her mother that "the old man Eaton had kissed her, and his face was as rough as a nutmeg grater, and did smell so dirty and horrid."

Her mother was scandalized and said:

"You must have said something wrong or acted bold, or he would not have behaved so. You are too big a girl to be kissed by the men. I don't see how Deacon Eaton could act so, and poor Mrs. Eaton lying dead in the spare room."

And Sara cried harder than ever, with words of denial so far as her conduct was concerned. And she added:

"I could tell a lot more about the way some other folks behave, but you wouldn't believe it, and would just blame me, the way you always do."

"Hush," said her mother: "I don't want to hear any more such talk, and you cannot go to the funeral now. That's settled."

"Oh, dear," said Sara, "and there's hardly ever anything going on here, and Mr. Seymour's going to sing at the church;" and stamping her little foot she screamed, "I just wish the old man Eaton had died instead of good Mrs. Eaton, and I *will* go to the funeral, so there!"

And she did go. Her mother raised her eyes after she was seated in church to take a furtive survey of the surroundings and encountered the smiling, triumphant face of Sara, which so discomposed her that afterwards she could not tell one word that the minister had said.

Four weeks later the grass was coming up in patches above the newly turfed grave where Mrs. Eaton's body rested in the little graveyard adjoining the church. The place still retained the look of a newly made grave, and could be seen even at a distance. One noted the fresh earth that was strewn about the plot.

At the old homestead where she had laid down her work there were many changes. Affairs were adjusted to the new housekeeper's ideas of propriety and fitness. The cows were milked each day, and butter made at regular intervals. The rooms were swept, and the dishes washed. If the quiet ways and patient attendance to duties had been missed for a few days, there was nothing to remind one of it now. Things had become regulated and the work went on quite as well, and the deacon said to himself "a leetle better, he thought, for Almiry sartainly was a leetle wasteful and keerless at times."

The deacon was spending much of his time before the looking-glass these days when he thought no one was round. The housekeeper had her eyes on him, and one day she heard him say in a low voice, "I can't see as I look so very old." She could read him like a book, and had her surmises in regard to what it was leading to, but she was too discreet to give voice to what was in her mind.

When she had come to take charge of the house a few days after Mrs. Eaton died, she had felt strange flutterings about her maiden heartstrings at the thought of what might come to pass, as she and the deacon were both single and eligible to marriage. But the deacon's manner had been so distant and aggravating that she had about given up all hope of holding any closer tie than house keeper, and she thought it likely that she might be out of a job most any time. And so she had grown sour and suspicious in consequence, with wits well sharpened for anything that would justify her suspicions. For she was certain, as she expressed it, "that the old fool was likely to take it into his head ter git married again, though for decency's sake, he orter stay single for a year."

However, the deacon had his own ideas in regard to propriety when it concerned his own welfare, and one night at prayer meeting (he nearly always led in prayer after the minister had opened the meeting) he prayed:

"Lord God of America, the Good Book teaches us that it is not well for man to live alone."

Everyone in the congregation knew it would not be long before Deacon Eaton would be looking 'round for a wife, if he hadn't already got his eye set on somebody, which was more than likely.

The deacon always insisted upon saying, "Lord God of America," just as if America was the only kingdom the Lord reigned over, and when the minister in a kindly way tried to correct him, he resented the interference as much as he dared to, and said "he guessed that he knew what was seemly, and that the Lord understood what was meant, and as far as he himself was concerned, he hadn't any interest in furrin parts." And as the deacon was set in his way, the minister had to submit.

The deacon missed his wife when he wanted to dress up to go to meeting or elsewhere. She had always combed his hair and put on his collar and cravat. And try his best, he could not make that old cowlick on top of his head stay down where it belonged. The first Sunday after his wife died he worked for an hour over it and was late getting to meeting, and then when he walked up the aisle to his pew, which was close up to the pulpit, he heard a girl back of him snickering, and he knew that old cowlick was probably standing straight up on the back of his head in the most aggravating kind of way. He had gotten the housekeeper to fasten his collar and fix the cravat for him, and he thought that he couldn't quite fetch himself to asking her to comb his hair.

"Whenever he got so flustered and bothered trying to get ready to go somewhere, he almost wished that Almiry hadn't died. And that hair business was one reason he had for thinking that he ought to get another wife pooty soon. He was sure that he couldn't continue to be so upset all the time."

Abby Ann Street, his housekeeper, heard him say "jest them words," for the deacon had a settled habit of speaking his thoughts out loud, and all the neighbors knew it.

So Abby Ann Street made up her mind that the next time that the deacon got dressed up she would just up and offer her services to brush his hair for him. She had her opportunity next day, for a town meeting was called and the deacon had to go. As he came out of the sinkroom with his hair all on end, she had the brush and comb in her hand and said:

"Now, deacon, your hair don't look nigh so good as it used to when Mis' Eaton was alive, and I wish you'd let me try my hand at fixen it."

"Wall," said the deacon, "Miss Street, I don't care if you do, for I'm free ter own up that thar cowlick beats me all holler, and my wife allus did fix it fer me, and that's why it comes so hard on me."

So that was settled, much to the satisfaction of them both.

The deacon's face got pretty red and Abby Ann's ears burned, for she could not help wondering what the neighbors would say if any one of them happened to drop in.

That was the beginning of a better understanding between them, and Abby Ann hovered about him, gaining his goodwill by bestowing little attentions that were like so much balm to the deacon's troubled spirit, for he always did hate to wait on himself, and never so far forgot himself as to do anything for any one else unless it looked like a paying investment.

Abby Ann considered that combing the deacon's hair had been a good stroke, a sort of putting another spoke in the wheel, and she was gaining ground. The household at this juncture was harmonious, everything running like clockwork.

But nothing lasts in this world and clockwork is apt to get out of kilter most any time, as Abby Ann could vouch for.

CHAPTER III

THE DEACON'S MARRIAGE

One day, like a bolt of lightning out of a clear sky, came the announcement from the deacon that he had serious thoughts about getting married again, and he thought it only fair to give Abby Ann proper notice to enable her to look out for another situation.

That afternoon the deacon put on his best clothes, and he fastened his own collar, and after a deep struggle managed to tie his cravat; after a fashion he also brushed his own hair. When he asked Abby Ann to do it for him, she replied in a snappish tone "that she had given up plying the barber's trade." The deacon went out of the house with his hair all askew and the cowlick on end.

Abby Ann peeped from behind the green shades at the window and saw him turn into the driveway that led to Raguel's house, and she wondered what it could mean. "What on earth," she said, "can be taking him there; she hadn't heerd as any of 'em were sick."

The deacon inquired at the house for Raguel, and was told that he would find him in the meadow lot. And he felt that fate was kind to him, for that was just the spot that he would have selected to lead the conversation into the channel he wanted.

After a few commonplace remarks had passed between them, the deacon cleared his throat and said:

"Brother Raguel, I wish we could jine our land at this pint. That thar meadow of mine that jines on this with the brook running through it would be a mighty fine piece of land all together."

"But," said Raguel, "I don't know as I want to buy any more land, and I don't care to sell any either."

"I know," said the deacon, and he looked shame facedly at Raguel, who was wondering if the deacon had dressed up in his Sunday clothes just to come over there to ask him that, "but I thought perhaps that you would give Sara to me, and then things could be settled satisfactorily to us both. I should like ter

marry the gal, and I dunno any reason why I shouldn't, nuther. I suppose it will make a stir and some talk in the neighborhood about the suddenness of it, but I dunno as I've got ter cut my cloth to suit other folkses' eyes. They don't victual, nuther do they clothe me, or nary one of us."

Raguel stood silent for a minute as if spellbound; then he turned on the deacon in wrath that was terrible, and said:

"You miserable old skinflint you, what do you mean by asking me for my little girl? Haven't you got any shame about you, you who are nearly old enough to be her grandfather, and everyone knows that you browbeat and half starved your poor wife to death? And now you are insulting her memory by talking of second marriage before she is cold in her grave. I think that you must be demented; that is the most charitable construction I can put on your conduct." And then as his anger increased he said: "I have thought a good many times that I was lacking in duty not to have you churched for the way you treated your wife. You get right off my premises, and don't you ever dare step foot on my land again. If you do, I'll have you took up for trespassing, neighbor or no neighbor."

The deacon went home, trembling with rage and discomfiture.

Raguel's folks tried to keep the affair secret, but in some way it got out, and the neighbors were all talking about it in less than a week. Mrs. Payson said "it was a wonder that poor Mis' Eaton did not turn in her grave at such goings on."

Abby Ann kept an eye out for the deacon's return, and she knew when she saw him coming with a red flush on his face, and noted how he raised his feet high from the ground, stamping them down again with a sort of precision that was natural to him when angry, that something was to pay. He closed the door with a slam-bang and shut himself into his bedroom, "and she reckoned that he had gone there to wrestle with that awful temper of hisn!"

When she called him to supper he came out looking meek and subdued, wearing his everyday clothes. Abby Ann had prepared an extra good supper and the deacon ate heartily, and as he arose from the table, he fairly beamed good nature.

The effect on Abby Ann was rather startling. She knew that the deacon was fond of good victuals and was always better-natured after he had been well fed, but she was not prepared for so sudden a change in his countenance. She wondered what it all meant, for he "sartainly had been awful mad over something." Her curiosity was soon to be gratified. The deacon fussed round the kitchen until the dishes were washed and put away. Then he spoke:

"Miss Street, won't ye set down a minute; I've got something on my mind that I want to say ter you, and I may as well speak right out and not heat about the bush all day. Will you marry me?"

Abby Ann said afterward "that she had allus bragged about herself being ekal to anything, but she guessed that she would have to allow that that episode fairly took her breath away, and beat all. And a child could have knocked her down with a feather. Thur was no denying that the thing was dretful sudden," especially after having been told a few days before that she must look out for another home. She was not lacking in spirit and she was not a fool, and as soon as she collected her wits, she replied:

"I suppose it's Hobson's choice with you, and I dunno as I'm so anxious ter git married as ter be obleeged ter take up with other folkses' leavings. For I know well enough that you've asked some one else ter have you and got the mitten, and I'm not going ter jump at the chance anyhow." And she walked away with great dignity.

Now, as I have said before, the deacon was stubborn, and opposition to his will simply fanned the flame, and if Abby Ann had been a finished coquette she could not have done better to lead the deacon on. He followed her as far as the door to her room, which she closed in his face, begging her to listen to reason.

After a time she came out of her room, but she was not at all disposed to yield. The deacon found that only by making a clean breast of the afternoon's occurrences could he expect anything like encouragement.

So he told her the whole story, and had the grace to add that he guessed he had made an old fool of himself, and if she would overlook it and stay on keeping house for him in the same economical way she had been doing, he would agree to give up all "idee of gitting married."

By this time Abby Ann was on the verge of hysterics, and burst out crying and sobbing and choking. The deacon was at his wits' end to know what to do to soothe her. Finally he did the best possible thing. Taking her in his arms, he said:

"Shoo now, I believe you do care somethin' for me arter all."

And Abby Ann allowed that she did, although she cried harder than ever, and between her sobs she interjected the words "that she would jest as soon be married as not."

The deacon thought it would probably put a stop to a deal of talk if they did get married right off—just as soon as she could make her arrangements. The preparations were speedily carried to fulfillment, and the marriage was more than a nine days' wonder, and as the deacon had shrewdly figured, stopped a deal of talk. The neighbors were divided in opinion regarding the story of the deacon's proposal to Raguel's daughter.

CHAPTER IV

SARA MEETS HER IDEAL

Sara grew more beautiful each day, and all of the young men for miles around were eager to pay court to her. On Sunday the little church was crowded with people, many of them coming from a distance to listen to her sweet voice. She led the choir, and her wonderful voice gave new meaning to the hymns that were sung.

She was not spoiled by the admiration that was so freely bestowed on her. All her life she had been accustomed to adulation and she accepted it as a matter of course, and her manner was natural and unassuming. It is the plainfaced, homely woman who loses her head and assumes airs when a little flattery is offered at her shrine.

At this time Sara had not seen any one of the opposite sex who appeared particularly interesting. When the young men made any attempt at lovemaking, she ridiculed and contemptuously held herself aloof from them. To her eyes they were the same freckle-faced urchins that she had grown up with—a little taller and larger, but as stupid, in her estimation, as ever. She could not separate them in her mind from her childhood days, or make it seem possible that they were grown up men.

She never told what her aspirations were, though it is probable that she had some sort of an ideal. Most girls do have, and in after years lose it—with other castles in the air that vanish into space when it comes to taking up a permanent residence for practical, everyday living.

The day was drawing near when Sara was to feel the soft fluttering at her heart, the quickened pulses, that proclaim a master-touch.

Her mother went one day to the church parsonage where the sewing society was holding its weekly meeting. A bed-quilt was on the quilting frame, and the women members of the congregation would be kept busy until supper time. In the evening the menfolks and young people would arrive, and the hours would be spent in playing games and in social intercourse.

Sara had gone with her father, as escort. She had just removed her dainty, pink hood before the looking-glass and was arranging her hair when she saw a smiling face above her own in the mirror. The face of a stranger, a boyish face with dark hair combed back from a white forehead and a pair of roguish eyes, was smiling at her.

She turned quickly, inquiring:

"Why, who is he? I never saw him before."

Out in the hall the young man was saying:

"There's such a pretty girl in there, boys. Tell me, who is she?"

The young men joked him, and the girls teased Sara, saying:

"You first saw him in the looking-glass, and over your left shoulder. He must be your fate."

"Yes," said Sara; "it's over the left—that's it."

Introductions followed later on. The young man had come from a distant city to make his home with his uncle, who kept the village store. He would assist as clerk in the store for a time, and if things went well, would become a partner later on.

Wallace Burr was different in his manner and bearing from the country boys, and Sara enjoyed his society. Before the evening was over it was evident that she had made a conquest and he had made rapid strides in his wooing. When the company dispersed he asked Sara's permission to walk home with her, and the two walked gaily away together.

Edna noticed the enjoyment that the young people had taken in each other's society, and she said to Raguel:

"Oh dear, Sara has surely got a beau, and now her troubles will commence."

And Raguel playfully inquired:

"Did your troubles commence when you had your first beau?"

"No, but Sara is different, and you know what the old woman predicted."

And then Raguel, who was usually the soul of good nature, replied:

"Lord Harry! do put that stuff out of your mind. You are always harping on what that old lunatic said. You act like an old guinea hen, Edna, though you can be sensible enough on other subjects, when that is not running in your head. No one can blame the girl if she does take to the young man, who appears to be likely looking. The Lord knows there's been enough of the other kind at her heels. The halt and the lunatics and the idiots have all been after her."

"Yes," said Edna, "and she'll most likely do as others have done before her—go through the woods and take up with a crooked stick at last."

"Well, she can take her time. I am in no hurry to get rid of my little girl, our one ewe lamb. It don't seem a day since I first saw her looking up at me from the old wooden cradle with those pretty blue eyes of hers that seem to look straight down into your soul. She is good enough and handsome enough for a king to choose."

Sara awakened the next morning in her little room under the eaves with eyes that saw nothing of her surroundings, although her mother, with tender sentiment that was uncommon in those days of hard, prosaic living, had picked a large bunch of the blue and white morning-glories that grew in a wild tangle about the garden wall, and placed them on the high bureau where she thought Sara would see them when she first awakened.

There was in Edna's heart a great tenderness for her little daughter at this epoch in her life. With her motherly intuition she had at once arrived at a conclusion, and thought she could foresee the end. She knew that the young man from the city with his wider experience and deferential courtesy was quite unlike the sons of the neighboring farmers, shy and uncouth in manners. She saw that Sara was attracted towards him, and felt in her motherly conceit that as far as external appearances were concerned he seemed a fitting mate for her beautiful little girl, whose dainty ways and graces were a source of pride to Edna, although no one ever heard her say that she thought Sara was beautiful. And when others praised her beauty, Edna always quoted, "Handsome is that handsome does."

Sara did not hurry about getting up. She awakened tired and languid, partly the result of the late hour of retiring and the reaction from the stimulating excitement of the evening's festivities. She was living over again the joy of a new experience, and a little tremor of delight passed over her at the remembrance of the compliments received from the young man, and her heart beat faster at the thought of seeing him again. For he had asked permission to call the following Sunday evening, and there was a possibility of meeting him before that time at one of the neighbor's houses. Little parties and impromptu dances were much in vogue at that season.

CHAPTER V

SARA'S FIRST MARRIAGE

Many hours of pleasant companionship followed, and in a few weeks Sara's engagement of marriage to Wallace Burr was called by the minister in the little church on Sunday. Three times the announcement would be made, as was customary at that time in the Protestant Church.

Edna was preparing the linen, and housefurnishing articles were brought to complete the dowry, or as they called it in those days, "a wedding setting out."

Sara would go to housekeeping. The old folks and young had agreed that it was best for them to have their own home nest and begin life's cares beneath their own roof-tree.

Down in the home lot the meadow pinks were blooming, bright red patches in the midst of green grass. Wallace and Sara walked there together, hand in hand. They rested by the stile to watch the beautiful coloring of the western sky where the sun had just gone down. Sara, with eyes up lifted, said:

"What a beautiful world it is, and I am so happy that it almost frightens me. Ever since I have been old enough to realize anything that feeling haunts me whenever I am particularly happy."

"What do you mean, dear?"

"Why this: No matter how much I am enjoying myself, in the background there seems to hover a something that tells me that my happiness will not last."

"But that is foolish, sweetheart, and morbid. We know that all things must have an ending, but that is no reason why we should not enjoy the pleasure while it lasts."

"I do not think that I am morbid, Wallace, for when things go wrong I try to make the best of it, and really it brings me greater happiness, for then I say to myself, there's surely something good in store for me after all this trouble is over."

Then they both laughed merrily, but there was a quiver in Sara's voice and a pathetic droop about the sensitive month that seemed to call for further explanation.

Wallace inquired:

"What else troubles you? I can see that there is something on your mind."

"Oh, I cannot tell you. It is just a presentiment of coming sorrow. You know the women of our family are subject to these attacks. Forebodings we call them, and they always foretell the coming of trouble. Something tells me that we shall be separated; there is a dark cloud hovering near."

"Now, dearest, listen to me and reason. That is all nonsense. What strange beings you women are. You are just tired out and nervous; so many wedding preparations have tired you all out, and upset your nerves. I shall be glad when it is all over and we are settled in our own little home."

And he tried to soothe her and banish all fears from her mind, while he kissed away the tears that were falling over the fair face. After a time Sara regained her composure, and tried to believe that she was just tired and nervous, and that all would end well.

Arrayed in her white gown, she went forth the next morning to the little church where Wallace awaited her coming. Many friends and relatives had gathered there to see her wedded to the man of her choice.

Wallace came forward to meet her, and as she placed her hand in his, he smiled and drew her arm tenderly through his own, saying a few words of encouragement, for the girl's face was drawn, and a strange agitation had taken possession of her. Together they passed up the broad aisle, as was the custom of the times, and stood in front of the old-fashioned pulpit, where the minister awaited them.

In after days Sara told of the awful fear that benumbed her faculties, and the words of the minister came to her as in a dream. As she mechanically made the responses required of her, the words seemed to her like the far-off echo of another's voice, and her own identity lost or usurped by some one else.

She rallied as the last words of the marriage rites were pronounced. Suddenly a strange sensation of chillness crept over her like the damp air from a tomb or underground enclosure, and she saw a mist of mirage cloud floating towards her. She raised her eyes to the ceiling, and there upon the white wall of the old church the vapory cloud separated and the shadowy form of Wallace appeared from out of the gray mist. As she looked, his right hand was upraised and waved slowly in her direction, and she distinctly heard him say, "Farewell." She turned towards Wallace in an agony of fear, and as she looked, he fell at her feet.

As in a dream, the people gathered 'round her, and she saw them raising the prostrate form and heard some one say:

"He must have died instantly."

All things after that grew indistinct and a blessed unconsciousness enfolded her.

When she was restored, it seemed to her as if she could not bear the terrible sorrow that had come to her. Three days later funeral services were held over the remains of Wallace Burr in the little church where a few days before he had stood a happy bridegroom by the side of the sweet girl-bride who had become all the world to him.

The childish face of Sara, shrouded in the somber crape veil, was as white as the face of the lover-husband who lay dead in his coffin. The heary mourning trappings looked out of place and unsuitable on the slender figure of the young girl, but custom and its requirements must be con formed to, or—"What would the neighbors say"—and the poor child was sincere enough in her mourning.

To Edna, her mother, the blow was a heavy one. Raguel's wise counsel and affection were all that kept her from breaking down. She said:

"The curse is working. That old woman was a witch, and all of her predictions are coming true."

As the weeks went by Sara regained her cheerfulness. When one has youth and health there are joys to look forward to, and time heals all wounds. To the aged, world-weary heart troubles weigh and crush; philosophy may uphold and patience be cultivated to bear, knowing that we must bow to the inevitable, but there is never the joyousness that is bequeathed to the young, who look forward and hasten with eager footsteps to greet the future that beckons them on, with flowery paths and fair promises, to the blessed City of Hope.

The months glided away one after the other, until two years were numbered with the milestones of the past.

Sara went sometimes to the graveyard and gazed upon the green mound that marked the last resting place of Wallace. She had not forgotten, but the past was a memory and no longer a poignant grief.

CHAPTER VI

SARA'S SECOND MARRIAGE

Sara had another suitor, although as yet he had not been bold enough to announce his intentions, but it was plain to be seen that he had come a-courting. She accepted his escort to singing school and choir rehearsals two nights in the week, and when one Sunday, at the close of the afternoon services, "he walked home with her right broad daylight," as the gossips said, it was evident that he meant business.

When the pussy willows came out of their hiding places to greet the little hepaticas as they peeped out of their furs, and the purple lilac bushes were green with budding leaves, just waiting for a little more sunshine warmth before shaking out their purple plumes, the village folks knew that Raguel's daughter was again to be given in marriage, and there was much speculation in regard to whether the wedding would be a private one on account of her being a "wider," or all would have a chance to view the bride in the church.

The white wedding dress was brought out, but Sara said:

"No, take it away, I can never wear that again."

So a pretty changeable silk was purchased and fashioned into a wedding gown.

Edward Royce, the prospective bridegroom, was the son of a well-to-do farmer, and was one of the number of boys now grown to manhood that Sara had engaged herself to when she was a little maiden just eight years old. The marriage was considered a suitable one, and Sara had been influenced to see it in that light. The young man's father had given him a well-stocked farm and a good start in life, with money enough for all current expenses.

Sara could not endure the thought of going to the church for the ceremony, so arrangements were made to have it performed at the parsonage, with only the immediate relatives as witnesses. The invited guests would gather at the homestead to await the return of the bridal party.

Sara and her parents were at the parsonage at eight o'clock in the evening of the day appointed. They waited in the parlor while the clock ticked away the seconds and minutes until half past eight. The half-hour struck, and still no bridegroom.

Sara had been chagrined at not finding him there when she arrived, for they had not been anxious to arrive before time, though her father had insisted upon promptness.

As time went on a growing uneasiness beset the waiting ones. At nine o'clock word came from the back kitchen, where watchers were scanning the roadway, that a horse with a boy clinging to his back was coming pellmell over the hill towards the house. He brought word that Edward was too sick to come, and he added:

"He wants the girl and her folks to come right off to his house, and the minister must come too, so they can be married. The doctor said that you had better do as he wants you to, 'cause he mustn't be worried."

The party started at once for the Royce farm. A few minutes after their arrival Sara stood by the side of the bed where the young man reclined, and the two were married. Edward grew calmer after the ceremony and, with Sara's hand clasped in his own, fell into a quiet slumber. He had begged her not to leave him, and there she remained by his bedside in all her wedding finery. Her mother waited in the room adjoining, with a heavy heart. Edward's mother sat near her with bowed head, and the stillness of death brooded over the house.

Raguel returned home where a few of the guests were still waiting. Bad news travels fast, and many of the neighbors had gone home when they had been told of Edward's illness.

At midnight the invalid awakened for a brief interval. He recognized Sara and a contented smile rested on his features. He made no attempt to speak, and almost immediately became unconscious.

The doctor had gone home, saying that the young man appeared to be resting comfortably, and would probably awaken stronger. As his services were not required, he would go, and come again in the morning. The watchers saw the change, and some one said:

"Get the doctor, quick."

Before he could be summoned the young man was dead.

For the second time in her young life Sara was a widowed bride.

CHAPTER VII

The Women Hold Themselves Aloof from Sara

The doctor said that Edward Royce had died of heart disease. The boy had not been very strong for sometime, but there had been no thought of serious trouble.

The old women in the neighborhood remarked "that perhaps he had growed up too fast." At the same time they shook their heads at one another and tried to look wise. Sara's position among them was not an enviable one. The women held themselves aloof. Although it was through no fault of hers that the two young men had died, a whisper had gone forth that she was in some way responsible, and they said:

"Who ever heard of two bridegrooms dying like that? There must be something wrong about the woman. I hope that she did not kill them, but it looks very queer."

There were mysterious shakings of heads, and when Sara went to church or any place where the people congregated, the older women looked upon her with stem disapproval in their faces, and the young girls giggled and sneered insultingly.

At first Sara was too stunned and saddened to notice their strange behavior. She could only wonder at the strange Nemesis that pursued her. She had never been a favorite among them. She was too independent in her manners and too attractive in features and form to be greatly beloved by her own sex, while the admiration so freely bestowed by the men made the women more antagonistic. There were many girls who were envious of her beauty and power to charm. The whispered innuendoes started by one of them fell upon rich soil and grew to greater dimensions as each girl or woman cultivated and sent forth the new seed, until at last the men began to look askance, not daring to show courtesy or kindness openly towards one whom the women had blacklisted.

When Sara fully awakened to the knowledge that she must have the added burden to her troubles of sneers and insults indulged in by weak, vindictive minds, it seemed more than she could bear. The torture this inflicted would have wrecked and destroyed the brain of a weaker woman. She thought it hard that girls and matrons whom she had never considered as her equals, or proper persons for her to associate with, should pretend that she was unclean in their estimation, and as they held their skirts aside as if fearing contamination, she wondered greatly. If her heart had not been troubled, she would have found it possible to laugh at such foolish exhibitions from such a source. Even the silly maids-of-all-work in the household whispered among themselves and grew disrespectful, saying:

"You are accused of strangling your husbands who died on their bridal eve."

The latent strength of character that belonged to Sara by inheritance sustained and upheld her, and she went about her duties quietly and patiently, ignoring the insults and frigidity of atmosphere that surrounded her. She had not given to Edward the absorbing love that had flowed so spontaneously towards Wallace Burr. His companionship had been pleasant and the shock of his death had made a deep impression; she was lonely and sad.

Edna's grief and anxiety for Sara's future were making a nervous wreck of her. She went about the house saddened and depressed, broken in health and spirit, convinced that fate held only misery and grief for her beloved daughter. The once happy home seemed destined to be a never-ending scene of sorrow.

Sara begged earnestly to go away from it all. She felt that she had become an eyesore to her mother, who would recover sooner without her blighting presence. For every offence against Sara brought hysterical attacks of grief to Edna, ending in ravings against the bitterness of the sorrows that they were compelled to bear.

Raguel consulted relatives in another town, and it was decided that Sara should visit them for a few months, or as long as she could be content to remain with them. The subject of past sorrows was not to be broached there, and among new acquaintances it was hoped that Sara would become like her old self.

The new life was pleasant. There were no young people in the house, but she made many acquaintances in the neighborhood. The only members of the household were her father's cousin Susan and her husband—a childless couple—and Sara became like a dearly loved daughter to them.

They were proud of the beautiful girl, and well pleased that she was so much sought after by the young people of the town. The young men paid her a great deal of attention, but she showed a preference for the society of girls and women, and was adored by them accordingly.

One young woman, Anna Lee by name, became her most intimate friend, and the two were often in each other's company. She invited Sara to go with her one day to visit relatives out of town, a pleasant ride of a few miles to the adjoining village. The drive was a pleasant one over country roads, and the girls went away in great glee.

The day was intensely warm. When they arrived at the house they were invited out to the grove. The house had been built in the woods and just outside of the clearing, the pine trees still clustered, making a delightful shade.

There were several young men at the house. Two were the sons, the other one a friend of the young men, lived in the vicinity. Anna had made a confidant of Sara on the way over. When the young men were introduced to her, she understood directly that the cousin's friend was the young man whom Anna had spoken of in terms that proclaimed more than ordinary interest on her part. The young man was a fine specimen of manhood, and at the first glance Sara thought him a perfect counterpart of Wallace Burr. The same laughing eyes looked at her with bright intentness, and the dark hair was combed away from the high white forehead.

Sara struggled for composure, and fought against the deathly faintness that almost overcame her. She could not explain to the interested lookers-on what her feelings were, and to their anxious questions replied that the heat affected her head.

The young man, Alvin Hills, looked embarrassed and nervous; he was sensitive and bashful, and had been quick to notice Sara's surprised look as she encountered his gaze, and it seemed to him that there must be something wrong about his appearance. To himself he acknowledged that she was the prettiest girl he had ever set eyes on.

Anna looked from one to the other in amazement, and as soon as she had an opportunity, she commenced catechizing Alvin, for the demon jealousy was awakened in her heart. She inquired of him:

"Where did you ever see Sara before to-day?"

The young man's face grew red, and he replied in a quick, resentful tone, "Nowhere." A sullen expression came over his face, and to the jealous eyes watching him it seemed proof of some kind of guilt.

Sara avoided him. She could not control her emotions, and felt that her only safety was in flight. There was a mutual attraction, but Sara was determined to fight against it, and the young man was loath to believe that he could gain the favor of one so far above him and superior to any girl he had ever met.

After their return to the house the girls followed Anna's aunt out to the kitchen for a quiet chat. Alvin's eyes followed their departure and watched the door eagerly for their return. The boys noticed his abstraction when a remark was addressed to him and guyed him. He paid no attention to them, and went home with his mind full of Sara.

The girls returned home next day. There was not much said by either. A restraint and coldness of manner seemed to be building a wall between them. Sara tried her best to appear natural and unreserved, but Anna would not unbend in her manner and held herself aloof.

The Sunday following, Sara went with her cousins to attend meeting in the next town, six miles away. As they drove up to the little church, Alvin Hills came swiftly towards them. He had stood in the churchyard with several of his friends when his attention was called to the approaching strangers, who were of general interest. He recognized Sara at once, and with fast beating heart at the thought of speaking with her again, he held out his hand to help her alight. And as her hand rested in his own for a second, the bright red blushes dyed each face.

Cousin Anson looked from one to the other and said:

"So you two are acquainted, eh? I think, young man, that I have seen you before to-day."

"Yes," replied Alvin, "I have seen you at my uncle's house. Amos Peck is his name."

"To be sure, and does he come here to meeting?"

"Yes," replied Alvin, "you will see him here. I saw him and the rest of the family go inside the church a few minutes ago."

Alvin invited them to the wide, curtained pew where his father and mother were already seated in their accustomed places. Alvin sat by Sara's side and found the hymns for her in the book they shared together. I doubt very much if either could have told—had they been asked—what hymns were sung that morning, for their thoughts were disturbed and running riot. When their fingers touched as Alvin turned the leaves of the book in his attempt to close it, the large hand closed over the smaller one, and the book fell to the floor with a loud, resounding thud. He felt as if all eyes must be upon him, and was in an agony of remorse at thus disturbing the meeting by his awkwardness.

There was a visiting time, after the services were over, in the churchyard. Cousin Anson was so well pleased with Alvin that he invited him to go home with them to spend the evening. The invitation was eagerly accepted, with a sidelong glance at Sara for approval. She looked anxious and bewildered, and when the opportunity came she inquired of him:

"Does not Anna expect you to her house to-night?"

He acknowledged that she did.

"Then you must go," said Sara, "I cannot allow you to stay here with me. No matter how much pleasure it may give me to have you here, I should be miserable afterwards at the thought of her disappointment."

She turned her flushed face towards him, and he, looking upon her bright beauty, felt that Anna's disappointment was of little consequence to him, and he would try to banish all anxious thought from Sara's mind if she would allow him to stay. He ridiculed the idea that Anna would miss him, but Sara was obdurate, and they finally compromised by his saying that he would go the later on.

After supper other callers came to the house, and although it was a little later than his usual time for calling, he went to see Anna. She met him with an angry scowl on her face, and upbraided him for his tardiness, and without half believing it, she said:

"I suppose you have been to see Sara."

And he acknowledged that he had.

Then the storm broke in good earnest. When the torrents of words ceased long enough for him to reply, he said:

"What a fuss to make over nothing." And as Anna had talked against Sara, he had made matters worse by saying, "The girl is not to blame, nor did I do anything wrong in going there. She came to our church with her people. I am acquainted with her uncle, and he invited me to go home with them. Not one of the party knew where I attended church, consequently there was no design or preconcerted arrangement to bring about the meeting. It just happened so, and no one is to blame."

Anna had allowed him to have his say. Then she drew herself up and with scornful mien looked at him for a full minute. He smiled and reached out his hand towards her. She waved him back, saying:

"Do not come near me—you are a hypocrite. All I have to say is that if you truly believe what you have said, then you are a fool. That girl found out from some one where you attended church, and prevailed upon her cousins to take her there, that she might meet you again and make even a greater fool of you—if it is possible to! The sly, sneaking thing! Or," with a quick, suspicious glance at him, "you told her the other day and asked her to meet you there, which I think very likely! And I can just tell you I do not believe that she is such a saint as she looks and pretends to be. Probably if we could know the truth, her people sent her away because she did not behave properly, and had disgraced them. I have always thought there was some other reason than her cousins' love for her or desire for companionship that kept her here for so long a time, and she an only daughter, too."

After a very unpleasant hour Alvin departed for home. Anna retired to her room with a grim determination in her mind that if there was anything to be learned against Sara's character she would ferret it out.

And before another Sunday had come, Fate, or his Satanic Majesty, had assisted her in her desires, and she waited with ill-concealed triumph for the time to come when she could bewilder and overwhelm Alvin with the story she had to tell.

Monday morning, after the washing was on the line, a neighbor who was a noted scandalmonger came to visit Anna's mother. The woman was a tailoress and had been to Kensington to make a suit of clothes for one of the parson's boys.

In those days a tailoress went about from house to house with a large pair of shears and a tailor's goose, making clothes for the old and young men of different families. Sometimes she was kept busy at one house for several weeks, or only a day or two, as the necessity of the case required.

Newspapers were scarce in those days, but they were not needed. One old woman and her companion goose more than filled the bill. She went from house to house fully equipped to astonish the inmates with "all she had heerd tell on"–the latest baby's arrival, and how soon another might be expected, though it is only fair to state that she did not accuse any "stork" with having a hand in the business.

She came prepared to make Mrs. Lee a long visit. "Work was dull, and she was willing to help about the house to pay for her keep, and tell all the news to bargain. And she guessed when some folks heerd what she could tell about some other folks, they would open their eyes some." And as Mrs. Lee looked sympathetic and interested, she could not contain herself any longer, and broke out with:

"I suppose you know that Sara a-visitin' at the Cowleses' house is a widder 'ooman, and not a girl, as they would like folks to think."

Of course the announcement was startling. And the "ohs" and "ahs" and "you don't says" were enough to satisfy the most exacting of story tellers.

"And what's more, she's been the means of killing two of the beootifulest young men as ever was. There's some sort of a curse hanging over her, likely to fall most any minute." And with a sly look at Anna, she said, "Some one we know had better look out."

Wednesday night Alvin, as was his custom, rode over to see Anna, and before he was fairly seated in the house had been told all the stories that were going the rounds about Sara.

Everyone in town had been in possession of the story for two days, for Anna and her mother had lost no time. It is needless to say that the scandal lost nothing by the telling, but was fast gaining in dimensions as it was passed from one to another.

Tuesday, Sara had gone over to the store on an errand, and had met several of the girls, who in response to her pleasant greeting had tossed their heads and looked the other way, and she concluded that she was to be ostracized on account of Alvin's attentions, and she made up her mind that when she met him again she would be more cordial and friendly.

Alvin had listened in silence while Anna related all that had been told her concerning Sara's character. She embellished where she thought a little fiction would make it worse, and as is often the case, said things that no sensible person could believe. Alvin concluded that the whole thing was an old woman's yarn added to by Anna's jealous spite, and he felt only disgust, although he was too diplomatic to say so. He made up his mind to visit Sara as soon as convenient, so that she might understand that he did not believe and could not be influenced against her by any gossip or unsavory reports. In the meantime he redoubled his efforts to pacify Anna, and she, misled by his behavior, thought that the affair with Sara had been nipped in the bud, and rejoiced accordingly.

The evening was more enjoyable than any preceding one since Sara had come upon the scene, and Anna felt that she had won the game. She had yet to learn the duplicity of man.

Alvin went home with his heart full of sympathy for Sara, and a great desire to see her filled his mind. He thought about it until it seemed to him that it was only Christianlike for him to go to her and by his tenderness of manner show that he was her loyal friend. The day following, her image still remained with him, and after the duties of the day were performed, he saddled his horse and started for Middletown.

When he arrived at the house, he found Sara in tears and considering the advisability of returning home to her father's house. All the chivalry in his nature rose to her aid. The true story of her troubles were related to him, and he anounced his intention to befriend and stand by her, if so allowed.

Cousin Anson and his wife were called from the room to see one of the neighbors "who had dropped in for a minute." Sara went quickly to Alvin's side and resting her hand on his arm, she said:

"I thank you for believing in me and for all of your kindness of heart, but I do not want to come between you and Anna, or interfere in any way with other friendships that you may have. Everyone here appears to believe me unworthy. I care too much for you to bring disgrace or unhappiness upon you, and it seems best that we should say good-bye. I shall always remember your goodness." The low voice faltered, and her cheeks were flushed like the delicate petals of the damask rose, as she reached out her hand to him in token of farewell. For one second her hand rested in his, and then he drew her gently to his side and folded his arms about her and whispered the one word, "Sweetheart."

The world and its sorrows, envy, and maliciousness for a little were forgotten. Then memory asserted its sway and she said:

"Oh! what have I done? What made you let me forget?"

And he answered:

"Darling, let me teach you to forget everything that is sorrowful, and remember only my love for you, which shall endure until death divides us."

With a shudder she withdrew herself from his embrace and turned away, saying:

"Oh! I wish you had not said that! Death will take you from me. I know that it will, for I am accursed. You must leave me now before it is too late. Go back to Anna and forget that you have ever known me."

"Hush, my little love, there is no going back. I love you with all my heart. I would rather die in your arms than to live apart from you with another. You must go home to your parents, and I will go with you and ask their permission to pay my addresses. Do not worry—all will be well."

Sara returned home, and Alvin's suit met with the approval of her parents.

CHAPTER VIII

SARA'S THIRD MARRIAGE

The home was gladdened by Sara's presence. To her the knowledge that she was in her rightful position brought happiness, and she became her radiant self again. Alvin came often to see her, and it was his desire that the marriage be speedily consummated.

Anna was nearly convulsed with jealous rage. Alvin had never been to see her since the night she had repeated the scandalous stories that the old tailoress had told them. She had heard of Sara's departure for home, and congratulated herself on the fact. In a few days the rumor reached her that Alvin had gone home with Sara, and it was a severe blow, but prepared her for the next news that the two were engaged to be married, and that Alvin went every Saturday to Kensington to remain over Sunday at the home of Sara's parents.

Anna waited several days with feverish impatience for some word of explanation from Alvin, but none came.

One day she went out to the open plain where the Indian settlement was. She had often been among them. An old squaw had made baskets and brought them to the house to sell, and in severe weather during the winter had come begging for food. She was a fortune teller, often foretelling events with such accuracy that many people held her in great awe and would not permit her to come on their premises, preferring not to hear of the good or bad luck in store for them. She generally foretold more evil than good, and wise people found it best to keep her at a distance.

Anna was a great favorite, and the simple gifts she brought with her were very acceptable. This day the old woman gazed at her in her stolid, expressionless way, but Anna said no word of her anxiety. As she arose to go, the old Indian inquired:

"Is the white girl much troubled?"

"Yes," said Anna. "Have you anything to tell me, Irene?"

A cunning look brightened the faded eyes, and the squaw arose and straightened herself erect. Pointing with outstretched arm towards the west, she said:

"Old Irene knows much that she may not tell. The White Lily has stolen your lover and robbed you of the love you hold dear. Men are faithless ever. The full of the moon looks down on an open grave, and the White Lily's mirth shall be turned into lamentation. The curse has not been lifted."

Nought else would she say. Anna went home in a saddened mood. If the Indian woman had said that the open grave was intended for Sara, it would not have been so bad, but the inference was that the grave was waiting for Alvin, and she could not endure the thought of his death.

On the way home she made up her mind to save him if it were possible. She watched several days for an opportunity to speak with him. At last she met him on the street, and, with tears coursing down her face, she implored him to be warned in time, telling him of the old Indian's prediction, and that she knew all would transpire as old Irene foretold.

He ridiculed the prophecy and was not affected by her tears. Anna turned from him at last in anger too deep for words.

At Raguel's house they were preparing for the wedding. Edna went about the house the reverse of cheerfulness, praying that all might turn out well, but she had *grave* doubts.

Sara would be married this time at home, and the old house was garnished and put in apple-pie order for the event. Relatives and a few friends and neighbors were hidden to the feast. Alvin had persuaded her to wear the pretty white gown she had worn the first time they had met. The wedding ceremony would be performed by the Rev. Mr. Andrews, pastor of the church where Alvin had been a constant attendant since his infancy, when he was taken there in his mother's arms.

The marriage took place shortly after sunset, and as the young couple joined hands, the full moon rose slowly over the hill, shedding its bright rays on the little bridal party, and illumining the room where the shadows had just begun to creep about the chairs and make fantastic figures—the reflection of each article of furniture that stood in straight, hard lines close against the whitewashed walls.

The guests were grouped in doorways and hall. On each face there was the expression of a strong nervous tension and agitation, and the silence was funereal in aspect. The solemn tone of the minister, the low responses, were listened to in an almost breathless attitude. As the last word of the service was spoken each head was bowed in prayer.

At the end the young couple turned towards the company to receive congratulations that were given in the heartiest possible manner. Alvin was in high spirits, and Sara's face was smiling. The supper was greatly enjoyed, and all was good cheer and jollity.

The minister stayed until a late hour, for the moonlight made the night nearly as light as day. He was the first to take his departure.

When his horse was brought out, saddled and ready for him, Alvin, without stopping for head covering, went slowly down the driveway with him, thinking that he would see him safely started on the roads twords home. He called back in response to an inquiry from some one in the doorway that he would be back in a minute, and then they passed from view hidden by the trees and shrubbery.

The old clergyman went safely on his way home, but Alvin did not return to the house where the guests and his bride awaited his coming. The young folks scattered about the house after a time missed him, and asked his whereabouts. Some one said that he had come in and gone to one of the upper rooms.

A half-hour later Sara descended from the room above, where she had been with two of her girlfriends, and asked:

"Where is Alvin?"

"Why, we have not seen him," they all replied.

"We thought he was with you."

Consternation fell upon them, until one of the young men said:

"He must be about the premises somewhere."

They shouted his name and searched the house from top to bottom, and then went to the barn and over every inch of ground surrounding the buildings, but they found no trace of him.

The women volunteered to stay the night out with Sara and her mother, while the men went out on the highway giving the alarm and forming searching parties. The neighbors came from all directions. The clergyman was sought and found quietly resting at home. He said that he left Alvin at the entrance to the lane. His horse had become restive and so they had not talked but a moment, and he had supposed, of course, that Alvin had gone back to the house.

For three days the men continued their search without finding a clew to guide them, for he seemed to have vanished from off the face of the earth as if the ground had opened and swallowed him, leaving no trace, and the only thing they could do was to abandon him to his fate, which would probably never be known. No one believed that he had voluntarily deserted his bride.

Sara had gone about the house with a set, hopeless look upon her face that was worse than tears. No one could realize the anguish that was in her heart. On the third day, when there were still no tidings and she was told that further search seemed useless, she had gone to her room, saying that she felt too sick to keep up any longer, and would try to rest. A few hours later her mother found her raving in the delirium of brain fever, and for many days her life was despaired of.

Sara's sickness and the constant care that she required kept Edna from selfish indulgence in grief, and, it is probable, saved her reason.

One day a party of young men out hunting found Alvin's body in a deep ravine. An Indian arrow told the cause of his death, which had probably been instantaneous. The arrow had pierced his heart. Without doubt, he had been killed shortly after the minister left him by one who was watching for the opportunity. His slayer had then taken the body to the deep ravine and covered it over with leaves and brush. In the woods where the Indians had been for months before the wedding day there was no sign of habitation— only the deserted wigwams.

Sara remained unconscious of all surroundings, and it was weeks after Alvin's remains were buried before she was in a condition to be told of his tragic end.

Anna went to the funeral and was carried from the church in convulsions. In a few hours death had set her spirit free.

Alvin was sincerely mourned, and a tide of sympathy went out towards Sara. All were horrified at the relentless fate that pursued her. At that time every one seemed to feel confident that she was not to blame, but alas, the tide will turn. The clergyman who preached Alvin's funeral sermon spoke of her as the innocent, modest young woman who was deserving of all sympathy and pity, and he prayed that her burdens might be lifted and peace granted to her. His words were repeated and for a time silenced the scandalmongers, who then fell in line and followed with the few who had always believed in and tried to sustain her.

CHAPTER IX

A Good Friend

Time passed on. Sara lived in quiet retirement. She found her greatest solace in wandering over the hills and through meadowland and grove listening to the meadow lark's song, the whistle of the quail to its mate. Down by the brook where the banks were shaded by the creamy dogwood blossoms was an ideal resting place. From the time that the cheery little blue and white hepaticas peeped out of the sodden earth in early April until the waving plumes of golden-rod and purple asters put on their somber brown robes in the late autumn her footsteps wandered through wood and glen, and sweet peace hovered near. Through the dreamy summer days the silence was broken only by the drowsy hum of the bees in the clover, the flutter of a bird's wing, or the cheery whistle, and these were like healing balm to the aching heart and benumbed senses. Mother Nature takes care of her children, and all who partake of her beneficent hospitality are granted new life and activity.

Sara's strong nature asserted itself, and she came back to her normal condition. She would never forget, but with patient resignation she accepted he decree, and determined that whatever new trials waited her she would bear with stoicism. With turning health came the natural desire for companionship—to mingle with other young people and join in their innocent amusements.

And that is as God intended life should be. We were not placed on this earth to mourn without hope. After our loved ones are laid away in the grave our duty is to the living. The dead may be safely trusted to God, who gave. He has the right to take unto Himself again. Mourning that inconsolable is in direct opposition to His will. Raguel had a friend, by name Asa Clarke. The two were about of an age and had been friends from boyhood. He had been a guest each time when Sara had been given in marriage, and a constant visitor at the house during her long illness–a good counselor and comforter through all troubles. He had been a widower for ten years, and it had long been settled by the village gossips that he would never marry again.

Raguel had often heard him say that no woman could ever fill the vacancy in his life and heart made desolate by the loss of his wife, and he looked forward to the time when he should leave this world of sorrow and join the love of his youth in a better land. It was, therefore, a surprise to Raguel when he told him that his heart had gone out towards Sara, and he was desirous of claiming her as a wife. He said:

"She is not like other girls after passing through such strange, sad experiences. She seems more mature, and although I am older than she by many years, you know that you can safely trust her to my care. I can wait patiently for her affection, and I believe that I can make her happy."

Raguel knew not what to say. At last he replied:

"She must not be coerced. I will put the subject before her, and it shall be as she wills."

When Raguel told Edna, she said:

"I think that he would make her a good husband, although he is too old for her, but I guess it won't make much difference, for he is not likely to live long after the ceremony. Have you ever told him about the curse? If not, then he must be told. Perhaps he will not care to marry her when he knows all."

"There you go again," said Raguel. "Why must you always harp on that fool story?

"Fool story or not" replied Edna, "I notice that it always comes to pass, and I fear it always will."

Sara did not rebel. She had a warm regard and respect for the elderly man who was always gentle and kind in his manner towards her, and she said:

"If he is spared to me I will try to make him a good wife and fill his days with brightness. I should be happy if I could look forward to peaceful days where wifely duties and homely tasks were the sum and total of my life, but I have grown distrustful, and feel sometimes as if it were better for me to die."

Her father went swiftly to her side and, taking her in his arms, said:

"Be of good cheer, daughter. God has not forsaken us. He will not let your young life be wasted. All will come right, and you shall find a safe haven of rest in a good man's love."

And thus it was arranged. Mr. Clarke was told of the old woman's prediction and the curse that was supposed to be hanging over Sara's head. He said that he was not superstitious, and was willing to take all risks, if there were any.

They would be married at the homestead, and start immediately for their own home, where all had been put in fresh order for the bride's coming.

Sara had gained many friends in the past year. She had been among the sick and aged people doing good, and wherever needed, by kind words and deeds had helped to sustain those who were in trouble.

Many came to offer good wishes and congratulations, and there were gifts from all quarters as soon as the engagement was made known. A few there were who held aloof, as might be expected there would be. Many of them began the old gossip, and as there are people who choose to believe evil rather than good, said:

"You needn't tell me there isn't anything wrong about that gal. Where there's so much smoke there's sure to be some fire."

Sara had one faithful friend who never wavered in her allegiance. Abby Ann Eaton, the deacon's second wife, had upheld and sustained Sara through all her troubles. The deacon had never spoken to Raguel or stepped foot on his premises since the talk in the meadow lot, but the women folks were friendly and neighborly.

Abby Ann made the deacon a good wife, and managed to hold her own with him. Shortly after her marriage she had been told "that the deacon would not give her enough to eat, and that she would never have a decent bonnet to go to meeting in." And she had made answer:

"We shall see what we shall see."

That was all, but the firm mouth settled itself in a straight line of determination that spoke volumes. There was no open revolt for several months. She was, as she expressed it, "gradually getting the reins into her own hands." And the time was drawing near when the deacon would have to knuckle under and submit to being bossed. He had ruled his mother and first wife until life had become a burden to them, but Abby Ann "calculated that he would not rule her."

CHAPTER X

ABBY ANN'S THANKSGIVING

Thanksgiving Day was drawing near, and Abby Ann wanted to keep the day in good, old-fashioned style. So one day she broached the subject to the deacon in this way:

"I want to make Thanksgiving this year, and I'm a-goin' to, too. It's a sort of religion with me. I heerd yer tell Squire Hastings that you'd had an unusually good harvesting, and it's only accordin' ter Scripter ter give thanks fer it, and share with them as hasn't eny too much of this world's goods."

The deacon's face got red and redder while she was talking. He was at the breakfast table that was set out in the back kitchen. As she finished speaking, he gave a kick at his chair, and with a final push sent it back against the wall. Turning his face towards her he snarled out:

"Yah, yah, yah! How a woman's tongue can run on. Thanksgivin' indeedy! I suppose that means a lot of sass and fixens, and my big turkey goblar thrown in, eh? Wall, I ruther guess not! Ye don't git it, not if I know myself. Do ye hear?" And the rough, red face took on a deeper color, while the bristling gray hair seemed to rise in a most vindictive manner as if to further emphasize his words. "Biled pot and a roast of pork in the oven was good enuff fer me and the fust Mrs. E. ter celebrate on, and I ruther guess 'twill harve ter do fer you. Do you hear?" And the deacon stalked out of the room, banging the door after himself.

Then Abby Ann remarked to herself:

"Yes, I hear, and much good will it do you, yer mean, pig iron, old cabbage-head. I almost wisht I'd died afore I'd had anything ter do with you, but seeing as I'm in fer it, I might as well be killed fer a sheep as fer a lamb. And as sure as my name's Abby Ann I'll circumvent yer, or die in the attempt."

Abby Ann was finding out that marriage may sometimes be a failure, even if one has a good home and a bank account.

She kept her own counsel, but preparations for a grand feast went slyly on. The best squash for pies and the best of everything else that could be abstracted from the market wagon was put away for use, until an improvised table in a private storeroom fairly groaned beneath its load of dainties.

The deacon, meanwhile, congratulated himself on his system of family discipline, and many times in the course of the day he said to Reuben, the hired man:

"Thar's nothin' like putten yer foot down and keepin' it thar where wimmin folks is consarned. I'm boss I am, mark that, will ye?"

A week before Thanksgiving Day, the deacon and Reuben went out to the poultry yard to make a selection of fowls to be sent to the city market. There was one turkey in the yard that was the pride of the farm, and the deacon said he "reckoned that air bird would ekal anything in the country fer size, weight, and quality." That turkey had been viewed and praised by envious neighbors until the deacon's heart expanded with joy every time he gazed upon it.

This particular morning the Grand Mogul strutted towards them, then staggered and fell lifeless at the deacon's feet. He picked him up a dead weight, all of his glory departed. The deacon sadly placed him on the ground and stood over him as if stunned by the calamity that had over taken him. As he pulled himself together, he said, "What on airth has killed him?" and he looked as if he had lost his best earthly friend.

Turning aside in agitation as he directed Reuben to bury the poor bird, he walked quickly away as if meditating on the awful "unsartinty" of earthly hopes and joys, saying to himself: "I dunno but that I made an idol of that air bird and am justly punished fer my consate."

When Reuben returned from the toolhouse with the spade he discovered that Mr. Turkey Gobbler defunct had disappeared, and he thought that the deacon had concluded to perform the last sad rites himself, and out of respect for the old gentleman's feelings he abstained from asking any questions.

Thanksgiving Day dawned dark and lowering, as Thanksgiving days often do, and Abby Ann said that "her neurology would not permit her to attend meeting," and she added: "As it's the only *new* thing I'm likely ter git, I'd better take care on it."

When the deacon expostulated with her, she snapped out:

"I've got ter tend to that pot bilin'," and she looked so cross that the deacon decided that he had better let her have her own way.

He went away mumbling, "that yer might well try ter turn the meeting house 'round as ter make an ugly 'ooman do anything she was sot agin." And he felt more than satisfied with himself whenever he thought how he had put his foot down on the Thanksgiving question.

Two days before Thanksgiving Abby Ann had called at the parsonage and invited the minister and his wife to take Thanksgiving dinner with them. The invitation was accepted, and it was agreed that they should come home with the deacon after the morning service. Reuben was told to wait for them and to say nothing.

The deacon was amazed when they took seats in the wagon. They were all smiles and evidently looking forward to a good time, while the deacon felt as if he were sitting on nettles, and as they drew near home, the perspiration ran down his back in rivulets at the thought of that Thanksgiving dinner of "pot luck" awaiting them.

Abby Ann met them at the door. All smiles and good cheer, she made them welcome, and after the preliminary greetings were over, ushered them out to the dinner table.

And *such* a dinner as it was. Parson Townley said to the day of his death that it was the best spread that he ever sat down to—transparent jellies, golden pumpkin-pie, honey in the comb, and fruit, all in true New England style— and nowhere else on earth can be found such excellent cooking, everything done to a turn. In the center of the table reposed a majestic turkey, done to a delicious brown.

When the deacon saw the turkey he nearly had a fit, and clutched at his cravat to loosen it. He gave Abby Ann one horrified stare, and then, as she reverently bowed her head, he did likewise, noticing that the parson was asking a blessing. That blessing was a blessing in more than one sense of the word to Abby Arm, for it gave the deacon a little time to cool off, and he hardly dared say cuss words in the presence of the minister, though Abby Ann was confident that he was thinking cuss words deep and strong, and she hoped the Lord would forgive him for it.

After the evening shades descended, and the parson and his wife had gone home, the deacon sought Abby Ann in the kitchen where she stood with sleeves rolled up, washing the best dishes and carefully putting them away. She rattled the tea things and made as much noise as possible, but the deacon had come to have an understanding with her, and he was not going to be put off. Going up close in front of her, he inquired in a solemn voice:

"Abby Ann, where did you git that turkey?"

And Abby Ann smilingly replied:

"I got that turkey from out of the Eaton poultry yard. I should ha' thought you would have recognized your old friend, the Grand Mogul. I am sorry ter say that I had ter git his royal highness as drunk as a biled owl, and before he had time ter sober up I had made a sacrifice of him."

She took another step towards the deacon, looking him unflinchingly in the eye, and said:

"All I want or expect is my just rights as the partner of yer bosom. And now I've got the upper hand, I callate that I kin keep it, do you hear?"—in exact imitation of the deacon.

The deacon looked cowed, and never answered back a word. And Reuben, who was listening while pretending to do the chores, chuckled to himself and mimicked the deacon's words, "I'm boss, I am; mark that." Then he nearly lost control of himself in a ha-ha. He went out to the barn 'and shouted, "Glory Hallelujah! the deacon's had ter knuckle under. I jest wish the fust Mis' E. was here ter see it."

Abby Ann, in talking it over afterwards with one of her friends, said "that she believed that when she told the deacon about the turkey, that only fer him having bin well fed, and consequently better-natured, he would have killed her."

CHAPTER XI

SARA'S FOURTH MARRIAGE

The beautiful June day, Sara's wedding day, was drawing to a close. All of the afternoon the neighbors had been coming and going, and all was serene happiness. The pastor of her church had united her with the quiet, elderly man who had won her affection and respect. At the close of the day the couple started for home. Sara never forgot that drive. The dewy air of the evening was sweet with the odor of blossoms. A new moon was looking down from a clear sky where the evening star was shining in all its brilliancy, and Sara exclaimed:

"What a beautiful world it is!"

Away in the distance they could hear the soft lowing of the kine. They stopped for a little rest where a stream of water glistened like silver between the rocks, hiding for a moment, then appearing lower down as it ran swiftly away to join the little brook at the foot of the hill. A grand night and a beautiful scene! A calm radiance and halo of peace surrounded them as they turned into the driveway that led to the house on the hill. Prince, the household pet, came barking and frisking to meet them, wagging his tail in glad greeting. The door was opened by the sister of the groom. She had been the housekeeper and companion of her brother since his first wife's death. As Sara advanced towards her, she folded her motherly arms about her, saying:

"God bless you, my dear child, and may you find peace and joy in your new home!"

After a slight repast the bride and groom retired to the room prepared for them.

Slowly the new moon went down beyond the hills. It was such a young moon that the hills reached up their green blankets of softest moss and covered it up close at an early hour. Prince, the dog, satisfied that his master had returned safely, had sought his own little house and laid down to rest.

Quietness reigned supreme, when a piercing scream resounded throughout the house, followed by another, until the whole place rang with the agonizing cries. Julia, the sister, hastened from her room on the first floor to the chamber above, and caught Sara in her arms as she sank into unconsciousness. She placed the quiet form on the bed that had not been disturbed, and hurried across the room to the low rocking-chair by the window, where she saw the rigid form of her brother quiet in death. She then turned her attention to Sara who was recovering from the fainting fit.

As soon as she could talk she said:

"I never thought of such a thing. He never complained of feeling ill. We had been talking and planning how we would remodel the house. He failed to reply to something that I asked him about. I thought he might have fallen asleep—the day was so warm—and I reached out my hand to his. It was so cold and dropped so strangely away from mine that I looked in his face, and I could see that he was dead. He had made no outcry. I was talking and I remember now that he had not spoken for some little time. Oh, what shall I do," she moaned. "I wish that I, too, were dead. He was such a good man—every one will blame me for being the cause of it, and turn aside from me again as if I were a pestilence. Oh, I must die before I bring any more trouble or death to any one else!"

"Hush, dear, no one can blame you. I have known for a long time that his days were numbered, and I was glad to know that he could find happiness with you even for a short time. He had been afflicted with heart disease for years, but he was so averse to having any one know or speak of it that I was enjoined to silence."

Morning dawned, and a messenger was sent to form Sara's parents, and after the fashion of the villagers, sowed the news broadcast.

After the funeral services were over and the family had returned to the house, they assembled in the best room to hear the reading of the will. An elderly man, arrayed in black clothes and with a stern visage, arose and declared that his late client had left a will. He then proceeded to unroll the heavy parchment, and in a sonorous voice read the contents. All personal property was bequeathed to Sara, with the exception of an annuity that should be paid to his sister, Julia Botsford. Half of the house was to be Julia's; if Sara outlived Julia, the whole reverted to her. He hoped that the two women would live together there in the old house in harmony. If Sara should marry again, or for any reason should prefer to make her home somewhere else, the two women could make any settlement satisfactory to themselves.

Sara decided to remain in her new home in compliance with her husband's desire, and she grew to love the old house, and she and her sister-in-law became firm friends, and very pleasant relations existed betwen them. And so the days and months passed by, filled with good deeds and many self-sacrifices on Sara's part towards others not so well blessed with this world's goods.

She felt that only by good deeds and alleviations of others' woes could the guardianship of the great property that had come into her possession be properly sustained by her as custodian. On every side one heard only expressions of respect and gratitude towards the young woman to whom no worthy person applied for aid in vain, and many others were helped that some people considered unworthy.

Sara knew what it was to be misjudged, and she held ever before her eyes the text, "Who am I, Lord, that I should judge her?"

And so for a little time Sara led a peaceful, happy life again. The days went by in quiet monotony, filled with daily duties faithfully performed—the life she had prayed for. And yet a little restlessness was creeping into this quiet Eden, and Sara ofttimes found herself wondering if the future did not hold something better.

CHAPTER XII

A Stranger within the Gates

One year from the time Sara had entered her new home there came a stranger within the gates. He had come from foreign parts, and claimed kinship with Julia and Sara's late husband. Julia was loath to acknowledge the relationship; although his claim and the genealogy seemed all right, she did not like the man. And she noticed that from the first moment he had set his eyes on Sara he had seemed to exert a strange influence over her, and his bold, black eyes followed her about the room in a manner that was utterly distasteful to Julia. She tried her best to have Sara see his faults with her eyes, but Sara only laughed and said:

"You are prejudiced because he is a foreigner. You must not expect him to appear like an American, for he comes from another land, and all people are not alike."

To Julia, his habit of smoking a pipe was abominable, and in her opinion he was altogether too fond of the cider barrel and brandy decanter.

Sara met all of her faultfinding with smiles and merry jests, and showed plainly that she did not view his habits in the light of faults, and she was flattered and pleased by his attentions to her. In one month from the day he crossed the threshold he told Julia that Sara had promised to be his wife, and he noted with great delight the chagrin on her countenance that she took no pains to hide.

Sara's parents had known nothing of what was going on. When Sara informed them that she had given her promise to the foreigner they were amazed. The knowledge that the Italian claimed relationship was bad enough. That Sara could for one moment harbor the thought of marriage with him was enough to make one's hair stand on end. Expostulation from parents or friends did no good. Sara seemed to have developed a wonderful amount of determination and self-will, and her mother finally came to the conclusion that it was only another form of the wicked spell that had entangled her in its meshes.

When the day for the wedding was set, parents and friends consoled each other by saying:

"All we can do is to hope that the curse will fall on his head and we shall be well rid of him. For surely God will not permit such a man as this foreigner with his wicked machinations to be spared, when good men have been cut down as by a scythe."

And so they waited.

All were bidden to the marriage. Sara showed no resentment because her actions were not approved. The rain poured in torrents, but people came from all directions to see the marriage. The ceremony was to be performed at five p. m., but long before that hour the guests had all assembled—curiosity, awe, surprise, and amazement pictured on each face, according to the disposition or temperament.

Sara was arrayed in pure white, and, at the bridegroom's desire, wore a veil that was draped and fastened in some sort of fantastic style around her head and face.

As the marriage service was in progress, it was whispered about the room that a stranger had just entered the house—a tall, dark woman who had come on foot from somewhere through rain and mud. She announced herself as the Italian's sister.

The minister had just said: "I now pronounce you husband and wife."

There was a confused noise, and people moved aside to allow the strange woman to advance. She hastened forward. As she reached the bride groom's side, she threw her arms about his neck, screaming sentence after sentence in the Italian language. The startled man tried to free himself from her embrace. As he succeeded in pushing her from him, she, evidently maddened by the rebuff, made a frantic rush towards him, at the same time drawing from beneath her wrap a sharp instrument, and with one lunge she buried it in the man's breast. Then, as he fell at her feet, she threw herself across the prostrate form, moaning and screaming and evidently pleading with him to give her some recognition. She was pleading to deaf ears. There had been only one convulsive shudder and then all was still in death. They summoned the sheriff, and the woman was taken to a temporary jail.

The day following it was found that the place was vacant. The woman evidently had assistance in her release. It is probable that one or more of her own people were close at hand. She was never seen or heard of in that neighborhood again.

Among the dead man's effects a letter was found written to "Carissimo." Enough of it was translated into English to understand that he had told her of his prospects, that he would soon have gold in plenty to lavish upon her, and in sunny Italy they would find happiness, with riches and honor for their old age.

That letter accomplished what nothing else had done, the enlightenment of Sara, and aroused all the spirit and sound common sense that had lain dormant under the glamor of infatuation. She put away all semblance of mourning, and in a shamefaced manner took up the duties of the house and tried to forget that the Italian nobleman had ever dawned upon the horizon of her life.

They buried him in one corner of the little graveyard, Sara paying all the expenses of the funeral.

This last marriage was only an episode. Sara acknowledged that she had been under a foolish glamor from which she had been rudely awakened. And it was with great thankfulness that she viewed the result. She might have met a fate that would have been worse than death. In after years she looked back to that time with consternation, and she often asked herself the question! "What could have ailed me?"

CHAPTER XIII

SARA'S SIXTH MARRIAGE

Cupid was preparing his darts again, and a man appeared at close range.

One day a young son of one of the neighboring farmers, "the only son of his mother and she was a widow," came to see Sara. He brought a large bunch of cinnamon roses in one hand, and a box of honey in the other.

Sara had known him from childhood. He had held aloof when others had come forward, after the little girl had grown to womanhood, although he had always kept a warm place in his heart for her. It was a small place, because he could not spare much. The cattle and farming utensils and all the farm property that he could accumulate took up most of the space, and his heart was not a very large one.

He had known that Raguel could not give his daughter a large dowry, and so he had been content to stand in the background and let others win. Now all that was changed. Sara had a good property in her own right, and was a desirable match. He had talked it over with his mother, who had been somewhat afraid that the ill luck that had befallen the others might come to him, but the money was certainly worth risking something for. And, as she said, Samuel had always been a healthy child and grown up as strong as an ox.

They considered the subject on all points before making any move. There was no other woman in the case, for he had never courted anyone. So he was not likely to be murdered by one through jealousy or for any other cause. His mother said "that he looked just like the Barneses,—was just the image of his father; and the Barnes family were notably long lived,—tough and hard to kill." And the money was so enticing. Samuel's hands fairly itched to have the handling of it. That was the way he expressed himself to his mother. At last his mind was made up and his mother counseled him to go ahead and win.

He remembered that Sara had been very fond of cinnamon roses and honey in the comb in her childhood days, and it stood to reason that she would be now—for what was a young lady but a little girl grown big? His mother sanctioned it all, and that was how Samuel went a-wooing—"sweets to the sweet," and roses to match the bloom in her cheeks.

The first time that he called was in the afternoon, on his way to the store. He wore his best clothes and his hair was greased in his best style. He had bought a new hat for the occasion, and had dropped it down on the floor by the side of his chair. Sara hastened to pick it up, but Samuel said in a lordly fashion:

"Let it lie there; the floor will hold it. It only cost five dollars."

Sara smiled when she saw the roses and honey, and said:"

"I see you have not forgotten my love for roses and taste for honey. The roses are beautiful. Your mother always has such good luck with her roses. Those on our bushes nearly always blast. I have not seen a perfect one this season. And white clover honey is a treat."

It was a fair beginning, and Samuel went home highly elated, shaking hands with himself all of the way there, and fairly beaming with satisfaction when he entered his mother's presence.

Why linger over the details? Before the supply of honey was exhausted, or the roses were dead, Sara was engaged to Samuel Barnes.

Her parents were averse to the marriage, and Julia tried to dissuade her from marrying so soon, for she hoped that by delaying affairs Sara might be brought to see things in the right light. For every one knew that Samuel was after her money.

"Mrs. Barnes was known to be one of the most mercenary women in the world, and Sam was a chip of the old block—scheming and crafty."

Sara was immovable. As on other occasions, it would seem as if opposition simply hastened matters. Her mother always said that it was the "spell" working, for on all other subjects Sara asked advice, and used good sense.

She went about preparing for the marriage without heeding advice or suggestions from her friends. Julia said, "You might as well talk to the wind." Sara thought that she knew her own mind, and that no one understood her. She was not shallow or fickle. A great desire to be settled in life dominated her, and a determination not to be crushed. She looked forward each time to a realization of her desires without believing in the superstition that she was accursed by an evil spirit. Her temperament and stubbornness of disposition would not allow her to give in or be governed by such a belief, although that belief was so deeply rooted in her mother's mind. Sara was of an affectionate disposition, and a great longing to love and be loved filled her heart, but she had yet to learn her own worth.

Samuel and Sara were married at the parsonage, and Samuel's mother was the only member of either family who witnessed the ceremony. The young couple were to reside with her until they arrived at a decision in regard to a home of their own. Samuel had in his mind's eye a farm that was for sale, and when the time was ripe he would approach Sara on the subject of funds to buy it.

They had driven eight miles to the town to be married. Samuel had harnessed up a frisky colt to the carryall against his mother's wishes. She objected to the proceeding because the colt was only half-broken, and its habit of kicking up its heels made Mrs. Barnes nervous and uncomfortable. Samuel said:

"Unless he could drive up the main street of the town in style there was not much use in going at all; he would rather walk. And he thought that would look pretty skimpy and poor, and would create talk."

They had arranged to stop at the house on the hill and take Sara in, and Samuel said that was one reason he wanted to drive the colt—so her folks could see what a fine horse he owned—and as for driving up there with the old mare for them to laugh at, he just wouldn't; "they would look great, with her old Sabbath day trot." So his mother had to give in, much against her judgment, for she said that she knew her heart would be in her mouth every step of the way.

The colt pranced off in fine shape, and Samuel asked his mother if she did not think they looked a good deal smarter than they would have done behind of old Sally, who was as tame as the house cat.

"Yes," said Mrs. Barnes, holding on to her bonnet with one hand and trying to still the fast beating of her heart by holding her other hand against it. "I'm thinking the smartest part of it will come when we get dumped out and our skin is all barked off."

"Don't you let that worry you," said Sam, and to show that he was able to handle the beast, he gave him a crack with the whip. Things looked interesting for a few minutes, but the colt quieted down after a while and behaved very well, coming to a standstill in front of the parsonage with a great flourish.

The wedding ceremony was over and they were ready for the return trip. Samuel untied the colt, and was about to help his mother into the carryall when the colt, made restive, no doubt, by having been kept waiting so long—for he had tried his best to pull up the hitching post—upreared and pulled hard on the bridle. Samuel gave the reins a jerk, and instead of speaking quiet, reassuring words, spoke sharp and loud.

That was too much for the colt's nerves, for he still held in remembrance the stinging blow from the whip. He raised his forefeet high in the air, and when they came down the young man was under them. The horse was now furious from fright and rage, and he pawed and stamped the ground until aid came.

When the horse had been soothed and quieted, ready hands had drawn the young man's form from the ground beneath his feet. His head was crushed and bleeding and he was unconscious, and remained in that condition until his death, which occurred a few hours after. Before the dawn of another day, Samuel's remains were lying in the spareroom at the farm house, where preparations were being made for his funeral. Thus another tragedy was added to the list.

No one could blame Sara for his death. His mother acknowledged to the neighbors that she considered the girl as innocent as a child unborn. She could solemnly swear to that on the family Bible if it was necessary, for Sara had no hand in his taking off and she hoped there would be no talk. She blamed herself for having urged him to marry. Though she bore no malice toward poor Sara, it did seem an awful pity that he could not have lived long enough for a child to have been born. Then some of Sara's money would "naterally" come into the Barnes family.

Parson Cowles, who had married the couple, was very kind and sympathetic, and gave Sara all the consolation at his command. Sara bore her trials with fortitude, and no word of complaint at that time ever passed her lips.

The minister continued his calls, and his interest in Sara never abated as the days went by, and she seemed to enjoy his society and brightened under his influence. He was a man of kindly disposition and greatly respected in the community. Of a quiet, studious nature, yet he had a hearty interest in life and all that was going on around him, and enjoyed the activity and endorsed all pleasures that the young people of his congregation indulged in. This was unusual in those days, when a long face and deep solemnity were considered to be the attributes of true religion.

At this period he was fifty years of age, and had never had much association with women. His congregation had long accepted the fact that he was not inclined towards marriage, and considered it a serious drawback to his usefulness. A minister needed a wife, and the good of the church required that he should have one. There were many kind and officious spinsters in the congregation who would have been quite willing to assume the duties that ordinarily fell to the part of the minister's wife and considered it no hardship, but he never asked them to.

His visits at the house on the hill were not commented on, for he had always shown himself sociably inclined and went about considerably, as was expected of a minister in those days, when the best dishes and preserves were brought out as often as once a month in honor of the parson's expected visit to supper.

CHAPTER XIV

Julia's Disappointment

Julia was always present when the minister came, and Sara often left them together, making a pretence of duties to be performed, until Julia, flattered by his attentions, had grown to believe that she was the attraction. Strange flutterings beset her mature heart in regard to him.

She had always held the secret conviction that she was cut out for a minister's wife, and with that sublime faith that is inherent in some female hearts, believed that kind faith would some day bestow the minister. It was now evident to her that her faith was to receive its reward. A becoming blush mantled her face whenever Sara left her alone with the minister, and her heart kept time to the thought:

"Now is the accepted time. Why does he not take advantage of the opportunity? Poor, bashful man!"

The parson only looked abstracted, and answered her speeches almost at random—another symptom, she thought, that he was badly smitten, and she did wish that he could gain courage enough to ask the momentous question.

The parson always remained on the occasions of Sara's absence from the room until she returned. Then with a patient expression on his face he would take his departure.

Julia never communicated her hopes to Sara, but there was a tacit understanding between them, and Sara thought as Julia did that he came to see Julia, and would eventually propose marriage to her, for such constant attention from a man of his age and position could mean only that.

Sara was not surprised when one day, after an unusually long call from the minister, Julia informed her that he had asked if he could come the next evening for a private interview. He had said that there was something on his mind, that he would like to say to her, and she also confided that it was her belief that affairs were about to be settled, and she wondered what sort of dress she ought to buy.

"And he had said that he hoped what he had to say would not surprise or shock her, because he placed great reliance on her good sense and judgment."

She had asked him to come early and take tea with her. Although she did not tell Sara in so many words that her company was not desired, Sara knew what was expected of her. So the next day she dressed early in the afternoon and went to see her mother, saying that she would not return until late in the evening.

Julia thought the parson looked sort of embarrassed and put out when shortly after his arrival he asked for Sara, and was informed that she had gone to visit her folks and was not expected back until late, and Julia added with an affected simper:

"I thought it would be so nice to set down to the table, just us two by ourselves, and so I did not try to keep her when she told me she guessed she would go out."

The parson's face flushed to a deep red color as he replied:

"Why, it seems strange that she should run away if she knew I was coming. You told her, did you not?"

Julia put on an air of pious demureness, saying:

"I do not believe in deceiving or trying to cover up things, and so I told the dear girl that you had asked the honor of my company alone—that you had something of importance to say to me. Was not that right?" And Julia spoke up sharp and quick, for she was a little bit nettled by the parson's manner and the way the conversation appeared to be tending.

"Yes," said the parson, "I think that I did make some such remark as that, but I trust there is no misunderstanding regarding it. I would be sorry to know that Miss, or Mrs.," (a little bit confused concerning her title) "Sara should be driven from her home on my account."

A silence seemed to fall upon them after that, and the supper that Julia had taken such pains with and so carefully prepared was scarcely tasted, and after a proper time had intervened, the parson called for his horse and rode sadly away without divulging the important declaration he had come so far to make.

After he had gone, a disappointed woman sat down by the cozy fire alone and reviewed the situation over and over in her mind, and she acknowledged to herself "that the whole thing beat her all holler. He surely had told her that he had something of a private nature to tell her. Then why in the name of goodness hadn't he told her? In her opinion an old bach was a queer thing anyhow, and she guessed womenfolks were not the only ones who were subject to changing their minds."

Sarah came home late in the evening and found that Julia had retired. She was surprised, for she had expected to hear a long account of "what he said, and what I said."

But no confidences were forthcoming, and she did not see Julia until they met next morning at the breakfast table. Julia had a look of embarrassment on her face and was very snappy in her conversation. When Sara inquired about the minister's visit, Julia retorted,

"If you want to know how he enjoyed himself, ask him."

She was mystified by Julia's behavior, but concluded to refrain from further questioning. She felt sure that she would tell her all about it when the spirit moved.

The days went by and the parson came no more to the house on the hill. At last Julia buried her resentment and sent word to him "that she hoped he would favor them with his company before long, and if it was agreeable to him she would be pleased to have him come to tea the next afternoon."

She waited feverishly for the messenger to return. The boy was a green farm hand. At last he presented himself with a broad grin on his freckled face, and to Julia's inquiry replied:

"Parson he told me first thing, was Mis' Sara to hum, and when I said yissir, parson he told me, then I'll come, Josh."

When Josh repeated his story to the other help in the barnyard, he added:

"Be-gosh, Miss Julia got as red about the gills as our turkey cock!"

Sara sat by the window knitting and never raised her eyes from the work in her hands until the boy had left the room. Then she looked at Julia and Julia returned the gaze with interest, and a hard, disdainful expression settled on her face, as in a sharp, rasping tone she said:

"Humph, I wonder if the parson is thinking about offering himself as a sacrifice! It beats anything what fools men are where a pretty face is concerned. My mother always said that beauty was only skin-deep anyhow."

It was the first hateful word that Julia had ever said to Sara. When she recovered from astonishment the tears flowed down her face and she hastily left the room.

Julia was sorry the moment after that she had said it, but it did seem so exasperating that the parson, with as much sense and learning as he had, could not see what was good for him, but must be so befooled by a chit of a girl young enough to be his daughter, when a woman nearer his own age more befitting to be a good wife stood ready and waiting to be had for the asking.

She could no longer close her eyes to the fact that the parson was bewitched over Sara, and that was the reason why he was so put out because she was not at home on the occasion of his last visit. And to think that he had had the impudence to ask the chore boy if Sara was going to be home.

"Well, if he wanted to make his bed in that direction, she supposed he could do it, but she would lose her guess if he did not find himself in his grave before he had time to think what was happening to him. Some one ought to warn him."

Sara remained in her chamber and her tears fell fast upon the pillow where her head rested. She made up her mind to go home to her parents' house and stay there for several days, for she was determined not to be in the house when the minister came next day. Julia could have his company all to herself. She would show her that she had no intention of intruding.

After a little time Julia came to her door and implored her to come downstairs. She paid not the slightest attention, although Julia said that she was sorry for the hasty words that she had spoken, and begged her forgiveness.

In the morning Sara went home to her mother. Julia had taken refuge in a fit of sulks, and as she watched Sara's departure said to herself:

"Let her go, and good riddance. I'll make the parson think that she went away because she hates him so, and maybe it will settle the whole thing and open the old fool's eyes for him."

Early in the afternoon the minister came, looking very dignified, and with elaborate courtesy passed the time of day, and, without removing his outer garments or taking the proffered chair, he asked for Sara.

Julia had not counted on such abruptness, and so she blurted out:

"She's gone home to her mother's to get rid of seeing you. There's nothing to hinder you from following after her if you are fool enough to do it!"

And then, almost scared to death at her temerity in speaking so to the minister—almost swearing at him, as she said to herself afterward,—she subsided.

The parson cast one withering glance at her and said:

"Misguided woman, you should pray to be delivered from that awful temper of yours or it will be your damnation!" Then he withdrew from the room and the house.

When Julia could collect her wits she went to the window and peeped from behind the shade just in time to see the parson riding swiftly away in the direction that Sara had taken.

The parson had not made up his mind exactly what was to be done, but he rode on until he reached the fork of the road. Then he drew rein and soliloquized:

"What a disagreeable old woman. It is clearly my duty to find a more congenial home for that pretty young girl."

Then, as he reached the turn where the four roads meet, old Dobbin came to a standstill. The parson with a touch of the reins said:

"We'll not take the road home, old fellow. We will follow the girl."

Dobbin made a hesitating halt, and then turned towards the home path, but the parson had made up his mind that duty—with the girl at the end on't—stared him in the face, and he was not the kind of man to turn back. Dobbin obeyed his command and took the long road.

CHAPTER XV

SARA'S SEVENTH MARRIAGE

Sara had said nothing to her mother of the words that had passed between Julia and herself, and her parents had never heard of the pastor's frequent visits at the house on the hill.

When he rode up to the door there was surprise and consternation. Sara met him all smiles and blushes, and without any hesitancy he accepted her invitation to enter the best room and make himself quite at home.

Raguel and Edna felt honored by the visit, and Raguel informed him that he was sorry that there was not time to kill a sheep for his inner man, but he would at once cut the head from a nice, fat hen, and there should be an excellent potpie made for his enjoyment. So the parson laid aside his outdoor garments and prepared to enjoy himself, well pleased with the welcome accorded him. The rest of the day was given up to feasting and visiting.

As the twilight shadows fell about them, the parson in the half-light, and greatly strengthened by his refreshments, told Raguel in a very feeling manner, "that it had come to his knowledge that the little girl was not treated as well by her late—or rather—Mr. Strong's, sister as she ought to be, and as he had become deeply interested in her welfare, he hoped that her father would give consent to the proposition that he was about to make. He had become attached to her and desired an early marriage to unite them, providing that Sara looked with favor upon his suit."

Raguel was very much gratified, but said that Sara must speak for herself.

Raguel called Edna and Sara and said:

"Let this be decided at once. He is a good man and must not be trifled with.

Edna was astonished to hear that Julia had been unkind, and was immediately up in arms and so excited that she scarcely paid proper attention to the minister's proposal. Sara quieted her, saying "that it did not amount to anything, a little ill-nature that would soon blow over."

Sara turned towards her father and said:

"I need no time to consider. If it is your wish, I will marry the minister."

The thought that Julia wanted him but that he preferred her was a great deal in his favor, and she felt that it would be a coveted position, for the minister's wife was looked up to, and could always have her say in the community.

The plans were all arranged before the parson left for home, and Dobbin carried a happy man back to the parsonage late that night.

Sara remained with her parents, and in the morning there was a family consultation, and it was decided that she would stay on until she should go to the parsonage as the minister's wife.

Her father went with her to the house on the hill to procure her clothing and other articles that she desired to remove. They had not counted on any opposition from Julia. When she heard what they had determined on, she begged and implored Sara to remain with her, for she was afraid the whole story would come out, much to her confusion, for what the neighbors did not find out they would surmise, and it would make so much talk that she would never be able to hold up her head again. "Sara should be mistress of the house and have everything her own way if she would only stay."

Sara was kind-hearted and Julia's abjectness excited her sympathy. And so it was settled that Sara would continue to reside with Julia.

There would not be a long courtship. The parson realized that the days were fleeting, and there was no time to lose. "He thought that six weeks was long enough to wait."

A few days after the engagement was announced he accepted Julia's invitation to supper, just to show her that he was too much of a Christian to hold resentment and, incidentally to get something to eat. He partook heartily of the good things Julia had prepared. She had put her best foot forward, feeling that she must do her level best as a sort of a penance for her past wickedness of conduct. The supper did not go begging this time, and later on Julia said to the kitchen help "that it did beat all, and was amazing, how these ministers who hadn't any wives to cook for them could stow away the victuals when they got where there was something fit to eat. For her part she didn't know where they put it all."

Julia was conspicuous by her absence from the supper table. She had told herself up to the last minute that she would put on a bold front and face the music, and then her courage failed her and she cut across lots to one of the neighbor's houses, leaving word at home that Mis' Williamses little boy had got the croup and she was needed over there.

She had heard in the afternoon that the child had a bad cold, and it came to her later on as a sort of inspiration that it would be a neighborly act to go over there with a bottle of goose oil, for Mrs. Williams was one of the kind that never kept anything in the house against a time of need, for she knew that her neighbors could always be depended on to have it. Mrs. Williams thought it was good of Julia to think of it and it gave the boy almost instant relief. It is needless to say that she was not greatly missed at the supper table, for Parson Cowles took solid comfort—between mouthfuls—in watching Sara's pretty ways and attention to his needs.

The wedding day was close at hand. Raguel and Edna had not been very communicative in regard to it, although they felt honored by the minister's choice.

The morning after he had spent the day with them, Mrs. Payson made an errand over to the house. Her curiosity had been excited by seeing a stranger ride up there, and she had kept watch all day, and knew that it was late at night when he went away. She could tell the exact minute by the clock, and it was too late to make any excuse over there that night. In the morning she did not wait to wash the dishes, but went right over to borrow a little soft soap.

She talked around, and heat about the bush without obtaining any information regarding the stranger's visit. At last, becoming desperate, she inquired: "If Mrs. Royce asks me who that man was that visited here yesterday, what shall I tell her?"

"Tell her that you don't know," said Sara.

Edna said afterward that it was so quiet there for a moment that you could have heard a pin drop. Then Mrs. Payson gasped, "Oh!" and started for home.

After that Raguel advised the folks not to say anything about it. "Let 'em find it out by their learning. It'll probably leak out after awhile."

And so it did. Sara and the parson were married in the little church where the good man had tied the matrimonial knot for so many members of his congregation. A clergyman friend of his came to officiate at the ceremony.

When it had become whispered about that the good minister was to marry Sara, it produced consternation on all sides. The history of her many marriages was discussed with bated breath.

The day before the one appointed for the wedding the old sexton was seen looking intently among the graves in the churchyard and when asked by some one who was passing along the road if anybody was dead, he replied:

"Not as I knows on. Ye haven't heerd the bell toll, have ye? But I don't mind telling ye that it appears to me that there soon will be, and I'm just considerin' where we shall lay the parson in case he dies as t'other uns have done."

The wedding day dawned bright and clear, and Sara, as usual, made a charming bride. Her dress was of pale lilac muslin, and there were beautiful plumes of lilac blossoms in her hair. She made a handsome picture. The clerical dignity of the bridegroom was softened by the tender smile that he bestowed on his bride; when he looked upon the lovely face his own brightened, and every one noticed and commented afterwards upon the glorified expression that illumined his face.

The marriage was performed without a break, and nothing occurred to mar the pleasure of the many guests who had gathered from far and near to witness it. The congratulations were hearty and sincere. The newly wed couple went out of church surrounded by admiring friends. They returned home with Raguel and Edna, where they were to entertain their friends. And it was a happy and contented party that sat down to the wedding supper at the old farmhouse that night. It was a late hour when the guests departed for their own homes.

The large front chamber at the farm had been prepared for the bridal couple. All had retired, although Raguel said that it was so nearly daylight that it seemed foolish to go to bed for so short a time, for folks in "ye olden tyme" were not given to turning night into day or day into night. And if merrymaking, or sickness that entailed watching with those so afflicted kept people from their beds all night, they were expected to be on hand in the morning and ready to take up the duties of the day.

Sara had been accustomed to taking a glass of water upstairs with her at night, for she often awakened during the night with a dryness in her throat and, unless she had the water, was annoyed by a cough. This night she had forgotten it, and had turned back to the stairway, when the parson insisted that he would go and get it for her. He was boyish in his eagerness to wait upon her. Sara said:

"I know the way much better than you do, and it is best that I should go."

In his desire to be gallant he would not listen and barred the way; at the same time, taking the lighted candle from her hand, he started towards the stairs.

It will never be known whether he was attacked by giddiness, or, being unfamiliar with the winding stairs, made a misstep. There was a sudden rush and the noise of a falling body.

Sara screamed and in a moment all was confusion. Tenderly they raised the body that lay at the foot of the staircase. One glance at the still form was sufficient to show that life was extinct. The poor man's neck was broken and death had been instantaneous. Strange fatality! For the seventh time Sara was a widowed bride.

She went to the funeral in her heavy mourning trappings. The curious glances bestowed upon her were hidden from her eyes by the heavy veil that enveloped her head and covered her face, but she felt the atmosphere of distrust that surrounded her, and partly heard several remarks that were audible enough to convey the impression that she was looked upon with suspicion. The tide had turned again.

She came away from the little church, saddened not alone by the deathblow, but burdened by the consciousness that, although innocent of any fault, there were people who would not hold her guiltless.

Sara was right. Her misgivings were to be verified. The talk went on in all directions. The ignorant people of the village shunned her as if she were a pestilence, and some proclaimed her as a witch. Her mother became fearful that in their ignorant superstition they might do her bodily harm, and she grew nervous and hysterical. Sara thought that she could read fear and abhorrence in her eyes and, grief-stricken and remorseful that she should have been the means of bringing so much trouble and sorrow to her parents, she felt that it would be best for her to go back to her home with Julia and remain there until her mother should become more calm and like her natural self.

Julia welcomed her with open arms and to her Sara confided her sorrows, saying:

"Never again will I allow any one to come a-wooing me, for surely it has been proven that I am accursed. A terrible Nemesis is following me," and as she rehearsed her wrongs, she became as one demented. Julia tried to console her, soothing and ministering unto her wants as she would have done to a beloved sister of her own blood. Sara refused to see any of her own people, locking herself in her own chamber when any one drew near.

Julia's old-time love for the girl had returned tenfold, and in the long weeks of suffering that followed it is probable that Sara would have lost her mind through much brooding and denial of food if Julia had not been so devoted in caring for her. She was untiring in her efforts to make Sara eat, preparing dainties to tempt her appetite giving her nourishing food each day, and insisting upon her taking a certain amount of it until, after a time, Sara resigned her will and turned to Julia as one whom she could trust, and no longer struggled against doing what Julia thought was best for her.

The time came when Sara was better in body and mind, and Julia had the satisfaction of seeing her return to a normal condition, and gradually awaken from the terrible lethargy that had engulfed her. Sara owed her life and reason to Julia, and as she regained her strength, she realized all that had been done for her; a great love for Julia entered her heart, and their friendship endured while life lasted.

CHAPTER XVI

SARA'S PRAYER

Sara went about the house again, much to Julia's delight.

The Rev. Mr. Bishop had taken the place as pastor of the Congregational Church made vacant by Mr. Cowles' death. It was he who officiated at the marriage, and had been the intimate friend of the deceased clergyman. He called to see Sara several times after the funeral, but she had on each occasion refused to see him.

He was a widower, and Julia was assiduous in her kindly regard for his welfare. He was impressed by her faithfulness towards Sara, and was flattered by the earnestness of her plea to him for advice. As the days went by he became a frequent visitor, and Julia felt that there was no mistake regarding the interest that was surely accorded to herself this time. One day her devotion was rewarded. The minister proposed marriage to her, and was accepted.

Sara was glad that Julia was to be made happy, and she at once carried out a plan that had been forming in her mind for some time; and so among the wedding gifts was a deed of the half of the house that had been willed to Sara. The house would belong entirely to Julia now. And Sara was happy in thus repaying to a certain extent the kindness and devotion that had been lavished upon her.

She took great interest in the wedding preparations. After the bustle and festivities were ended she had her effects removed to the house of her father, where she felt that her presence was now needed. Her mother was feeble and her father needed her companionship. With renewed strength she felt capable to battle again with fate, although she hoped that she might lead a quiet life and become a comfort to her parents in their old age.

Julia was sincere in her endeavor to persuade her to continue to live with her, but Sara had determined to go to her own people and minister unto their needs, trusting to find peace and happiness in attending to the humble duties that awaited her.

In going back to her old home she had not counted on what was before her. As soon as she appeared among the old scenes she found that bitter trials were to be met that required more than human courage. She was compelled to submit to insults on every side. When she went out people passed her with averted faces, and in many instances where two or three were together words of reproach were spoken loud enough for her to hear. The death of her late husband, the good and well-beloved clergyman, had stirred up all the old feeling against her. Even the silly maids in her father's house were disrespectful.

The situation seemed unbearable and she was tempted to take her own life. She was sorrowful, for she felt the reproach that was cast upon her. And she said:

"I am the only daughter of my father, and if I do this it shall be a reproach upon him, and I shall bring his old age with sorrow to the grave."

Early teachings gained the victory. She remembered that there was One on whom she could lean: He who knows our sorrows and our need holds out His hand to each and every one who turns to Him in prayer. Then she prayed towards the window and said:

"Blessed art Thou, O Lord my God, and Thy holy and glorious name is blessed and honorable forever. Let all Thy works praise Thee forever. And now, 0 Lord, I set mine eyes and my face towards Thee and say, take me out of earth that I may hear no more reproach. Thou knowest, Lord, that I am pure from all sin with man. And that I never polluted my name, nor the name of my father in the land of my captivity. I am the only daughter of my father, neither hath he any child to be his heir, neither any near kinsman nor any son of his alive to whom I may keep myself for a wife. My seven husbands are already dead and why should I live? But if it please not Thee that I should die, command some regard to be had of me, that I may hear no more reproach!"[1]

At the same time another tortured soul was praying. He was Tobit, a distant kinsman of Raguel's, who had become blind and had much trouble. And the prayer ascending to God's throne was like Sara's, a supplication to be taken from earth where he was misunderstood, grieved, and unjustly reproached. He prayed:

------

[1] Tobit, Chapter III.

"O Lord, Thou art just and Thy works are mercy and truth, and Thou judgest truly and justly forever.

"Remember me, and look on me, punish me not for my sins and ignorances, and the sins of my fathers, who have sinned before Thee;

"For they obeyed not Thy commandments, wherefore, Thou hast delivered us for a spoil and unto captivity, and unto death, and for a proverb of reproach to all nations among whom we are dispersed.

"And now Thy judgments are many and true. Deal with me according to my sins and my fathers' because we have not kept Thy commandments, neither have walked in truth before Thee.

"Now, therefore, deal with me as seemeth best unto Thee, and command my spirit to be taken from me, that I may be dissolved and become earth, for it is profitable for me to die rather than to live because I have false reproaches and have much sorrow.

"Command, therefore, that I be led into pleasant pastures away from the rugged paths that hold only thorns."

Beyond the darkest clouds there is light. When we totter along, crying out in our helplessness that there is naught but grief and torture in this life, and we can no longer do battle where failure seems assured, yield not—look upward and beyond; somewhere God's light is shining and in His own time and way its rays will fall fair and beautiful across our path, warming and giving new life to each stricken heart. Resignation and patience are the lessons all must learn, and blessed hope; when the way is darkest we know not how soon His promise shall be fulfilled—we have only to wait. The heart that is lonely and grief-stricken to-day, ere the rising and setting of another sun may have gained joy unspeakable.

Raguel found much comfort these days in Sara's companionship, and Edna regained her cheerfulness. The household had settled down into quietude. Sara did not go abroad much. The strain of meeting old associates and having them look askance at her was more than she could bear. So she remained at home, only taking necessary exercise about the grounds, and helping her mother with the household duties.

One day at the noon hour when all was bustle and preparation—for the midday meal was in progress —a stranger was seen advancing towards the house. Raguel had watched the moving figure coming over the hill and had said:

"That must be the squire's son. I heard that he was home from foreign parts."

Edna and Sara had been attracted to the window by Raguel's exclamation, and were trying to get a view of the young man. At this juncture he left the path for a shorter cut across the green lawn. The movement was characteristic of the young man, who never lost any time getting to a place by taking the longest way round. He stopped just before he reached the door, and with a pleased smile on his face drew in a long breath of the spicy, pine-scented air. Afar off, over the hills, behind the screen of stately pine trees, the crows were cawing—not in the loud, hoarse tone that greets one in the early morning, but in a soft, drowsy fashion that told of hunger appeased and a secure refuge beyond the sentinels that so safely guarded them.

It was an inspiring scene that his eyes beheld. Rugged and grand on either side of "Cat Hole Pass" arose a pile of rocks; here and there a feathery mass of foliage grew from out the rocky groves that encompassed them on either side, a wild tangle of light-green shrubbery and darker shade of pine needles drooping their pretty fringe in the heat of the sun's rays, and sending out odors that were health-giving balsam to all who came within range of their beauty.

The young man was good to look upon, tall and stalwart, with keen blue eyes, and as he raised his hat from his head to enjoy the summer breeze, one noted the noble brow, where the dark hair clustered in little, soft rings. The face showed firmness of character and kindliness of disposition, a face to be trusted instinctively.

The large dog that lay stretched at full length beneath the lilac bush got up and shook himself, then lazily advanced to meet the young man, who reached out his hand to receive the big paw that was laid confidingly in his clasp. Prince never made any mistakes in regard to his acquaintances, and it was evident that he desired to add the young man to his list of friends. Animals have a clear insight to human character, and the man or woman that a dog or cat runs away from is not one to be trusted.

As Raguel had surmised, it was the squire's son, John Mildrum, and he came with a message from the squire—business connected with the state militia, and not to be trusted to one of the farm hands.

When the squire's wife heard him tell John what was required of him she had called him aside and asked if he realized that he might as well send the boy into the lion's jaws as to that house, and she said she thought a man of his age and experience, with children's welfare to guard, ought to have more sense. As for her she could foresee what the end would be, and he would see the consequence of his foolishness when his son was lying in his coffin.

The squire thundered out:

"What do you mean, woman, by such tomfoolery?"

"I guess you will know what I mean fast enough when you see your son in the toils of that woman who is possessed by a devil! And," she added, "he will have only his father to thank for it."

The squire said:

"I can't make out head or tail of what you are driving at."

"I suppose," said his wife, "that you never heard tell of Raguel's daughter and the seven husbands that she has had, did you?"

"Well, of all the tarnal fools, women are the worst," said the squire. "Do you ever think of anything but making matches, or unmaking them? As if it were any sign that he would lose his head because other men have! My son is made of different stuff and knows what is expected of him. I'll risk his ever making a fool of himself, losing his head over a farmer's girl. It's a wonder you did not worry over him when he was away for fear he might bring home a bride from one of those heathenish countries where he sojourned for so long."

Sara opened the door for the young man, with no especial interest in his coming. The little coquettish airs that had been so natural to the girl a few years before were gone, and a settled expression of sadness brooded over the fair face. She looked at the world with the same frank, fear less eyes, but they seemed to question whether she was to be greeted with kindness or meet averted glances—the resigned manner of one who has known the trouble of bearing unjust censure and criticism. It speaks well for the sturdy nature that through all of her troubles she had kept a sweet disposition. She forgave easily and did not become soured or morbid over the insults received from the venomous, small, narrow-minded, ignorant people who attended their church services each Sabbath and yet had never been taught to "Judge not, that ye be not judged."

Small communities are hard places for people who have any individuality of character to live in; a woman of refined tastes and a natural desire to hold aloof from the tittle-tattle of narrow minds and gossiping tongues of idle neighbors who have more time than brains at their disposal, is at once looked upon with suspicion and treated accordingly. It is an unspeakable horror to be brought in contact with the spitefulness that becomes a second nature to many a countrywoman who, if she cannot find out all of her neighbor's business, immediately jumps to the conclusion that there must be something wrong where there is anything to hide.

To be popular in the country village "you must be one of us." You must ask your neighbor's advice when you desire to entertain company—or set a hen! Some excuse must always be given for your conduct, "or what will folks think." If you so far forget yourself and your duty to the community as to refrain from discussing all of your private affairs, you are under ban. Anything that savors of secrecy is wrong, and the culprit pays the penalty.

Sara was pure and good, also beautiful to look at. That alone was a sin not easily forgiven by her traducers. A terrible fate pursued her. As one after the other of her husbands had been taken from her, dying almost at the altar, people had wondered, become horrified and startled, and, although nothing regarding the circumstances at tending the deaths had been kept secret, there were many who said: "There must be something wrong about the girl,"—bright and beautiful Sara, with that mysterious, magnetic attractiveness that made all men her willing slaves, and so brought down on her defenceless head the ire and abuse of many ill-natured and envious women, who repeated one to the other the words of the silly housemaids "that she must have strangled her husbands or poisoned them to death."

"For you know," they said, "that it is not likely that all of them died natural deaths;" and they drew aside their soiled skirts in righteous (?) indignation that so fair a face should dare to show itself among them.

Sara had no designs upon the squire's son. She greeted him in a calm, dignified manner. He had heard of her troubles and was glad of an excuse to go to the house and see her. She was a little girl when he went away. He remembered her as a prim little maid in a long-sleeved gingham apron that was always running over with kittens. Now as he looked at her, he noted the same graceful turn of the head, quick and birdlike, and several times while he was talking he caught an amused glance from her eyes that vividly recalled to his mind the little girl he had known in the past. He had not been very well acquainted, because she was bashful in the presence of the big boy who was the son of the proud old squire, the richest man for miles around.

John refused the hospitable invitation to have dinner with them, but said that he would be pleased to come again if it was agreeable to them. He would like to show Sara some beautiful shells that he had picked up in his travels. He remembered seeing her once when she was about five years old, with her little hands full of snail shells that she had picked up down by the brook in the meadow. She had shown them to him very solemnly, declaring that they were beautiful, and that she had brought them a long journey from over the sea. The memory of it all came back to him as he sat there talking to her father, and he looked with greater interest at the girlish figure, and sweet face with its delicate pink and white complexion that reminded him of the dainty coloring of the sea shells.

After the young man had gone Raguel said:

"The squire's son has grown to be a fine young man, just as smart as his father is without the stern, cold manner that made the elder man so repelling."

Edna sighed and Raguel turned suddenly to look at her, trying to catch the expression on her averted face. Edna would not look at him and, as if fearing an interrogation, she hastily left the room, and Raguel, who was not given to jumping at conclusions, felt that perhaps Edna was right if, as he supposed, she was anxious over the outcome of the association of two young people well calculated to become life partners. And he thought:

"It would never do, never! Why, the old squire would pull the house down over our heads. He would never give his consent to such a thing, or countenance his coming here. Surely Sara will not encourage him, knowing that marriage with him would never be sanctioned. Even if no curse were hanging over her head"—and Raguel acknowledged to himself that there was—"the squire would look amongst the gentry for his daughter-in-law, and very likely has in his mind's eye a choice."

Then Raguel arose, putting away his meditations. He took up his interrupted work, and in a petulant voice said:

"I must be getting into my second childhood or old-womanish to harbor such thoughts. There is nothing to be done, as I can see, but to let matters take their course. I am not going to forbid the young man to come here, and I cannot lock my little girl up, or envelop her in a veil. She is modest and sweet enough for a king's son to mate with, or better still, she is good enough to be the wife of the best American in good New England, and hang it all! I am not going to interfere with her happiness. She has had trouble enough that I could not ward off, and I like this young man."

It was nearly a week before John came again. Sara saw him coming. He had crossed the lot and swung himself over the low stone wall instead of going round by the road. He brought with him a small casket of foreign design and workmanship, a beautiful little workbox, and it was filled with lovely rose-tinted sea shells.

Sara had never dreamed of such splendor, and frankly showed her admiration in the prettiest possible manner. Among the treasures were pieces or sprays of red and white coral. Sara's delight stimulated the young man to give her further pleasure by relating where he had picked up the different shells, and telling her wonderful stories of the natives and their characteristics in the different countries he had visited.

Thus the hours sped by until it was supper time, and he remembered that he was expected home at that hour to meet company who came by his father's invitation, and, as he suspected, had been invited for his especial benefit.

CHAPTER XVII

The Lady Sophia's Visit

Lady Sophia Ainslie and her aunt, the Lady Charlotte Ainslie, were coming to make an extended visit.

The Lady Sophia was the daughter of an Englishman whom the squire had become acquainted with abroad. The young woman was past her first youth, and was not at all attractive. She was short in stature and broad in figure, with long, corkscrew shaped curls hanging over her ears, framing a face that reminded one of a full moon. Her manners were affected and silly, and she behaved in the way that is often assumed by a maiden who has outgrown her kittenish days, but seems to think that if she kicks up now and then and acts frisky that it will be attributed to youthful exuberance of spirits. They seem to forget that "Father Time" has left his marks, and that the demure behavior of a matured pussy-cat would be much more in keeping with their years.

The squire had often spoken of his son to Lady Sophia, and after the manner of a proud father had been lavish in his praise. The squire seldom talked with any one at any length without mentioning his son, and every one knew that John was the apple of his eye. Lady Sophia had always been a good listener, and the squire felt that she was an appreciative one. When the squire threw back his head and straightened his shoulders to-say, "My son is a very exemplary young man, and has never caused me a moment's uneasiness by his conduct," one felt that the young man must be more than ordinarily good.

Lady Sophia was not wealthy. She had a small fortune that had come to her when her mother died, the remnant of an ample marriage dower, and she dwelt in a beautiful ancestral home. The elegant style of living had impressed the squire, and he believed that so much luxury must mean an unlimited bank account.

The squire had one other child, a little daughter named Ruth. The child was born deformed—a hunchback. Her health had always been delicate. She was at this period fifteen years of age, and in size resembled a child of ten. Ruth had overheard her father telling her mother of the anticipated visit, and that he hoped John would take to the young woman, saying:

"An association with a genteel woman like the Lady Sophia would be a great help to any young man. And I don't see how any young woman in her right senses could help liking a fine young man like our John. I count on your aid in having my wishes carried out," added the squire in his most pompous manner.

Ruth loved her big brother and was jealous of his affection. It had always been given to her in unstinted quantity from the moment that he had taken her in his arms when she was three days old. His heart had ached when he saw the little crooked back as she grew older, and he was told that she would always be deformed. The big boy had mingled his tears with his mother's, and in his heart had formed the resolution to always care for her and make her life as pleasant as possible.

Ruth was bright and forward in speech, with a sarcastic tongue that was the delight of her father and the horror of her mother, for she was sure that it would make enemies for the child. She had the elflike countenance that one so often sees accompanying that deformity of figure. Her eyes were bright and sharp, seeing all there was to be seen, and her keen intuition seemed to read the thoughts of those about her, and as she accredited most people with hypocrisy and malice, she was considered uncanny and witchlike. She had greeted the Lady Sophia with a little short nod of her head and had placed her hands back of her waist when Lady Sophia had reached out her own hand to shake hands with her. As she was a privileged character, no apparent notice was taken of her behavior by the other members of the family.

An intense dislike towards her took root in the shallow mind of the Lady Sophia, who expected every one to bow down and worship at her shrine. Instead of ignoring the childish action and trying to win the girl's regard, she said:

"You must be a bad-tempered child, and I would just like the training of you."

Ruth was furious, and she retorted:

"Are you a trainer? That's what father calls the soldiers. Did you take part in King Philip's war?"

All this was said smilingly, and apparently in great innocence. Lady Sophia's face was red enough, as Ruth said afterwards, to infuriate a bull.

Lady Sophia had been told that John was devoted to Ruth, and if she had been wise, coming as she did to storm the fortress, she would have had the tact and diplomacy to win the girl's regard, or at least to make an effort in that direction. As it was, war was at once declared between them, and she would have a hard time trying to make Ruth lay down her colors.

Since John had returned from his travels he and Ruth had been almost inseparable. They had resumed the old-time walks of her childhood days. When she was a baby, scarcely old enough to go about, he had taken her for long trips through the woods over hill and dale. When the little limbs grew tired she had continued the journey in his strong arms. There was complete confidence and the greatest affection between the two, and it was the fear of interruption in this comradeship that had antagonized Ruth. Then when she heard what her father's plans were, the advent of the strangers grew detestable.

She was a wayward, undisciplined child; because of her delicacy and infirmity, she had been given her own way too much. She had a kind heart, and she was easily governed if one knew how to go about it. Like the old squire, she worked by the rule of contrary. She resembled her father in looks and disposition.

John had hastened home when he realized how late he was and his duty to his father's guests. He came forward to greet the visitors with a pleasant smile and cordial welcome. Tall and erect, he looked to be a king among men.

Lady Charlotte bowed low before him with the sweeping courtesy that was the custom of the day. Lady Sophia followed her example, and with a simpering smile replied to his inquiries regarding her health and the pleasantness or otherwise of her journey.

At the supper table Ruth inquired:

"Jack, where have you been all of the afternoon? I looked everywhere for you. I wanted you to hear me say my lesson before I could call myself perfect," and she turned a surprised pair of eyes towards him as he hesitated a full minute before replying.

Then he said:

"I had an errand to do," and his face grew red.

"Ah," said Ruth, "you must have been up to some kind of mischief, or you would not blush so over it."

All eyes turned towards John, and his mother's sternly spoken, Ruth," made the young man laugh, and he said to Ruth:

"You ought to know all about it, little monkey, for you are always in mischief yourself," and he slyly shook his head at her as she opened her lips with the evident intention of pressing him for an answer.

His mother noticed his embarrassment and quickly arrived at the right conclusion regarding it, and through her mind the thought ran, "He has been to see that girl. The Lord help us all. I knew just how it would be, and I can see how it will end. And to think his own father sent him there as if he desired to offer him up as a sacrifice. Now he has started on that track there will be no turning back."

When Jack went up to his room Ruth followed him there. She plied him mercilessly with questions until he, knowing her disposition, felt sure that the wisest course would be to tell her the truth without any evasion. So he made a clean breast of it. She looked very thoughtful while he was talking, and she noted that he expected her approval, and she said impulsively:

"She is real sweet looking and I do not wonder at your liking her," and she added; "I suppose all young men have to fall in love sooner or later, and I would rather have you marry her than the Lady Sophia.

"I looked for you when she came. I was peeping from the garret window and when she got out of the carriage she showed her legs, and you can't think what a sight they are. They look for all the world like rolling-pins, only not as large. Maybe that is why her face looks so much like dough."

"Now do not be ill-natured, little sister."

"Well, I don't care, I do just hate her, Jack, I do, so there! What do you think she said when I told her that I could not find Jack? She turned up her nose and asked, 'H' and wat his Jack? Your dog?' And when I told her that Jack was you, she answered, 'Hi should think John was much better a name than Jack for a man.' I think that she is simply 'orrid'" (aping the young woman's accent to perfection) "and I'll never put any more wood shavings on my head to make believe I have curls again, after seeing those corkscrew abominations on her head."

"I thought I heard you say once that you adored curls," said Jack.

"So, I did, sir. I doted on them, but I am cured for all time on. Don't you ever dare to marry her, sir," and a small finger was held up in admonition. "I happen to know that—you need not laugh—father has made up his mind that you are to marry that awful-looking old maid, though he always pretends that it is only old women who try to make matches for folks."

Jack laughingly assured her he had no intention of marrying anybody at present, and she had better leave such important matters to older heads, and not be silly about things that were never going to happen.

The next afternoon when the ladies retired to their rooms, Jack brushed himself up a bit and started across lots to see Sara. Ruth was entertaining a small maiden from the village, and he felt entitled to a few hour's pleasure of his own seeking. He found Sara in her favorite seat beneath the old sweet apple-tree. The girl made a pretty picture in her white frock amidst the green foliage of the shrubbery. As she raised her eyes, he caught the look of pleasure that told him he was welcome.

They were only drifting. He had not made up his mind to anything except that she was sweet to look upon and her society brought satisfaction and contentment to him. She was happy, feeling that there was nothing to worry over as long as he did not declare himself a suitor for her hand.

Her father had considered it his duty to tell her after John's first visit to them that she must keep always before her mind the fact that the young man would probably be governed by his father in his choice of a wife, and as the old squire was known to be very proud and to hold lofty views in regard to his children, that he would never consider any one outside of the gentry good enough for an alliance with his family. In the squire's eyes education and refinement counted for nothing unless there was money enough to sustain a position. In his heart Raguel had no sympathy with the purse-proud aspirations of the squire.

Sara had heard of the guests at the big house, and when John spoke of them, she eagerly noted that he did not appear to be overwhelmed by their grandeur, or at all eager to court their favor. He said, after a few words concerning them, that he didn't know how long they expected to stay, but he hoped they would go before they wore their welcome out. This was said with a humorous expression on his face.

Sara was never tired of hearing about John's travels, and the pictures he drew of the different countries and the customs of the people were of absorbing interest to her.

Lady Sophia had been at the squire's house ten days when the squire followed John out in the yard and began a conversation with him on the subject of marriage, in what he considered a very circumspect manner. John smiled indulgently at the old gentleman. He remembered what Ruth had told him of his father's views and plans for him, and was prepared for what followed. As he made no reply to the squire's discourse, his father concluded to come to the point and tell what was expected of him. He said:

"My son, it is the desire of my heart to see you married. You are close on to thirty years of age, and it is time that you were settled in life with some good woman for a partner. The Lady Sophia would make you a good wife, and I should be proud to welcome her as a daughter."

John knew what to expect if he thwarted his father's wishes, and that the squire's violent temper would make a scene that was utterly distasteful to him; and yet he felt that the question should be settled at once and for all time, for he knew that not under any circumstances would he ever consent to marry the Lady Sophia. So he said:

"Father, I cannot do as you wish. I have no feeling for the Lady Sophia that would warrant me in carrying out such a proposition."

The squire was in a towering rage and shouted loud enough to be heard a mile away:

"Zounds, sir, what kind of feeling do you expect to have towards a respectable lady? Eh? Feeling be hanged, sir. She is a lady of high degree and a proper person to be the mother of your children. What more do you want, eh?"

At the sound of the loud voice Ruth came hurriedly down the walk, and as she instinctively raised her eyes to the front of the house, she caught a glimpse of ringlets and a flutter of the curtain as it fell in its folds again. And she said:

"Father, the Lady Sophia is at the window listening to you."

She could not have said anything more strategic to terminate the interview, but the end was not yet. The flames would smoulder, and John knew that they would break out again at the earliest opportunity. His first thought was to escape it all by leaving home. He was not dependent on his father. He had a good business interest in the city where his money was well invested in shipbuilding. The squire had given him a goodly sum of money when he had attained his majority—"to start him in life," he had said. The money had been well invested and the young man was in good circumstances.

He did not care to be driven from his home—and there was Sara. When he thought of her, he felt that he could not go away from the pleasant association that had become a part of his everyday life.

His father had returned to the house, but he saw little Ruth sitting in the garden, her head resting against a bench in evident dejection. He joined her, placing his arm about the small figure, and he asked: "What is it, dear?"

And she smiled as she raised a tear-stained face to his own:

"Oh, Jack! I almost know that you will give in to him, you are so kind-hearted and good-natured, and mother says, 'that you are too easy going,' and I guess, awful as it sounds, I would rather see you dead than married to that putty-faced old image! I heard Miss Allen, my teacher, say one time that old Squire Mildrum was an awful tyrant. And that is as true as true can be, if he is our father."

John tried to soothe and comfort her, but did not succeed, until after a time she brightened up long enough to inquire if he was willing to swear on the Holy Bible that nothing should induce him to marry the Lady Sophia.

He tried to persuade her to take his word for it, saying, "You know that I never told you a lie in my life," but she was too shrewd to accept that, and she insisted that he should do as she wanted him to, for Ruth had been born with the same obstinacy of disposition that belonged to the old squire. At last Jack allowed her to bring her Bible, and he solemnly took his oath that he would not wed the Lady Sophia Ainslie. Then she was satisfied and inclined to be indulgent. Smiling at Jack she said:

"I suppose you think that I made you do that just to have my own way, but that is not true. I did it for your own good and protection, for I am pretty sure with that as a safeguard. Father cannot talk you over and break down all barriers that you raised in objection. I know his ways, but now you are under oath, and you cannot go back on that. Even Father wouldn't want you to do what you had sworn not to."

CHAPTER XVIII

Deacon Eaton 'S Revenge

The squire ordered his horse saddled and started for a ride to calm his ruffled spirits. He drew rein in front of Deacon Eaton's gateway—not because he wanted to, for his own thoughts were all the company he cared for. He stopped in response to a signal from the deacon who had seen him from his vantage ground in the meadow where he was mending a fence.

Now the deacon had had something on his mind to do for several days. The main thing was to see the squire, but he could not bring himself to the condition of going to the big house, knowing, as he did, that there was company there, and he acknowledged to himself "that it was a ticklish subject to tackle any way you might look at it, and he didn't see how he was going to get speech with the squire." So when he saw the squire riding towards him he felt that it was a special dispensation of Providence.

Abby Ann had noticed the deacon's abstraction for a week, and that he talked to himself more than usual—and that was in his case a sign of mental worry. She had not been able to draw him out in any way, although she tried by repeated questioning.

As the squire stopped, the deacon approached him and said:

"Walk your horse back a-ways, Squire, as far as the home lot, and I'll jine ye in a minnit;" mysteriously adding, "I've somethin' of importance to tell ye, and I dunno as thar's eny use of letting the wimmin folks into all the secrets. The goodness knows"—with a snarl—"they know more than is good fer 'em now!"

The squire followed the deacon's instructions. The deacon stopped at the shed for a handful of nails—"to sort of allay any suspicion at the house," he said.

He could see that the squire was irritated, for he wore an expression of sternness and impatience, and he said to himself, "The old feller will feel wus when I'm done with him."

He commenced the conversation in his usual way by quoting Scripture. Rolling his eyes heavenward, he repeated:

"Man who is born of woman is of few days and full of trouble."

The squire was in no humor to listen, and he sprang into the saddle and was about to ride away, exclaiming:

"If you are going to preach a funeral sermon, deacon, I guess I'll have to be going."

The deacon look chagrined, but placed his hand on the bridle, saying:

"Ye'll be sorry, squire, if ye don't listen. It's about that son of yours;" and he blurted out, "mebbe ye don't know that he spends all his arternoons with Raguel's darter, lolling under the trees, and worshipping of her as if she were one of them hethin idols we've heerd him tell on."

The squire was dumbfounded. He despised the deacon and he had too much pride and self-respect to unbend in any way before him. The small, malicious eyes watching his face could not see he yond the mask of cold, impenetrable dignity. The squire made no reply. He remained a second or so as if waiting for further disclosures. As none were forthcoming, he touched the horse lightly with the reins and rode on. Over the stern face a darker shadow fell, and be fairly hissed these words through his closed lips:

"So there is where the trouble lies. Well, we shall see if a farmer's daughter with an unsavory reputation is to hoodwink a son of mine. By the Lord Harry, I will crush the whole lot of them under my heel first."

As the squire rode away the deacon brightened up, and with one of his characteristic chuckles said:

"That's the time I killed two birds with one stone. I guess I've squared things with Raguel, and I've taken a leetle of the high and mighty techiness out of the squire."

Abby Ann had watched the little byplay at the gate and had know that there was something to pay. So she dropped all household duties and followed the two men by a short cut to the meadow, keeping in the background. She was not near enough to hear the conversation, but she inferred from the attitude of each that some startling information had been given by the deacon and that the squire had ridden away in anger. She joined the deacon on his way back to the house, and inquired:

"Now, what were you saying to the squire?"

The deacon felt new courage coursing along his veins since he had vanquished the squire, and be bristled up and answered:

"I dunno as it's eny of your business, but I don't mind telling ye, since ye're so inquisitive, that I considered it my bounden duty to tell him about his highfalutin son's goings on with Raguel's darter, and I guess it was a pretty bitter pill fer him to swallow," and a gleeful expression rested on the old wrinkled face.

Abby Ann did not stop to pick her words; as she turned towards him her voice rang out loud and clear:

"Your duty, you miserable, old sinner of a hypocrite! Your duty is to mind your own business. Didn't any one ever teach you that? And you a perfessor of religion, too! A deacon in the church! It almost makes me wonder if there is a God when I see how you are allowed to go on in your sinfulness. I wonder that He does not strike you dead. How do you dare pray to Him?"

And as her anger increased, she said:

"I'll be dumbed if I ever listen to your praying again—anyway, I won't until you repent in sackcloth and ashes. To think of you hounding that poor child after all the trouble she has had, and through no fault of her own either. And now you have set that domineering old devil of a squire on to her. Get out of my sight, you cur. Go to the tavern for your dinner; I'll be squelched if I get a dumb thing for you. No, and I wouldn't if you were starving to death before my eyes."

And she was as good as her word. The deacon went without his dinner that day, and it was many a day before she would stay in the room when he was holding prayers. She gave up going to church, although the deacon told her "that she was carrying things too fur," and begged of her to go "if it was only jest fur the speech of people."

The squire when he reached home went straight to his own room and summoned his wife to his presence.

"Maria," said he, "do you know that *my son* visits Raguel's daughter day after day?"

"No," replied the mother. "I did not know, but I am not surprised to hear it if it is so, and I want you to bear in mind that *you*, his father, sent him there the first time that he did go there, and you have only yourself to thank if harm comes of it. What else could you expect? He is only human, and Raguel's daughter Sara is a beautiful girl. I told you just how it would be, but you always think that you know more than anyone else does, and no one can ever tell you anything. John is a good son, and much as it troubles me to say it, I think you had better let matters take their course now, for it is too late to meddle. You will never be able to force John to do anything against his will. It may all die out after a little time if there is no opposition, and no harm done."

The squire's anger was getting beyond bounds. Astonishment had kept him quiet for a few minutes, for it was the first time in all their married life, that his wife had had the termerity to speak up. He sprang from his chair roaring:

"Silence, woman! Zounds! Did I ask your advice? Hold your tongue. If he had a mother who had the sense of an idiot she would have governed and tutored him, and things could never have come to this pass. You have given him his head all his life and indulged all his whims, and now you can see the result. You listen to me, woman, and you can tell him just what I say. I have made up my mind that he shall marry the Lady Sophia, and I am not to be thwarted. As her husband, he can take his place among the highest in the land. I didn't waste good money on his education to have him marry a low-down farmer's daughter. And unless he accedes to my wishes and breaks off going to see Raguel's daughter, he shall never cross my threshold again. Nor will I ever own him as son, or give him one cent of my property, even though he goes begging from door to door and dies in the poorhouse."

"Don't be a gander, squire. When he is your age he will in all probability be worth more property than you are. I guess he won't go a-begging this week or next with such a fine business as he has and money in the bank to his account. Now I've listened patiently to your tirade, and I mean to have my say for a few minutes and you are bound to listen.

"You mark my words, John will not marry the Lady Sophia. No, not if she were the last woman on earth. Nor would he receive my blessing on the union if he did. For of all the selfish, disagreeable women I ever came in contact with she is the worst. I don't know how her Aunt Charlotte ever puts up with her tantrums. I am sure that I couldn't. Poor thing, I am sorry for her.

"And I can tell you this—unless Lady Sophia packs up her duds and takes herself away from here pretty soon, I am going to tell her that her room is better than her company. She looks almost as old, if not quite, as I do when you see her without her frumperies, and I don't know what you can see about her that you could expect a young man to like. Maybe you would like me to step out, so that you could pay court to her, but I'm not a-going to do it, nor is my son to be pestered or driven to commit any foolishness, or be turned out of his home. If he does go, his mother goes with him.”

Then she grew hysterical and said:

“I’ll have the law on you and that Lady Sophia if you carry on in my house. I’m your lawful wife and you can’t help yourself.”

Then, suddenly coming to her senses, she stopped talking and looked at the squire, who stood as if transfixed, looking at her in wide-eyed amazement that did more than anything else could have done to bring her to a state of calmness, and she resumed in a quieter tone:

“I don’t often speak my mind to you, squire, and every one knows that you rule your family with a rod of iron, but the worm does turn sometimes, and that is what has come to pass with me. I’ve been put upon by you all of our married life, and I am getting where I would like to have things a little bit my own way once in a while before I die.”

The squire did not recover his speech, but continued to gaze at her as if he thought she were demented. She waited a minute. He did not speak, so she left the room. As she stepped into the hall, there was a rustling sound of moving skirts, and she was in time to catch a glimpse of the Lady Sophia as she whisked into her room. The sight was like the waving of a scarlet rag in the face of a bull. She turned back and re-entered the room where the squire stood, and with eyes that were fairly blazing with anger said:

“If that woman has any decency she will not remain where she is not wanted, and if you do not find a way to get rid of her—I will!”

The squire was alarmed over this new difficulty. He ejaculated:

“Of all the tarnal nuisance women and children take the cake! A man might as well try to live in a hornet’s nest, but since I’ve started on the war path I’ll fight this thing to the bitter end.”

In the afternoon of the following day he rode over to Raguel’s farm, and demanded in his sternest and most domineering manner to see Sara. Raguel refused, saying:

“I am her father. You can have no business with her that cannot be transacted with me.”

“Very well,” said the squire. “I am told that my son comes here a-courting her, and I want it stopped. He has given his promise to a lady of high degree, and I won’t have him mixing up with any common truck.”

Raguel advanced toward the pompous old fellow, who receded, placing a chair in front of himself. Then Raguel controlled himself enough to say:

"I never thought the time would come when I should turn you out of my house, squire. But I guess you had better go now before my ire gets the better of my reason. I have no control over your son. If you have, why did you not say all this to him, and not come here to insult your neighbors?"

And at the thought of the indignity offered to them, Raguel advanced towards the squire again, and said:

"Who are you to give orders to my daughter? My advice to you is to get right out of here and out of my sight as quickly as you can."

The squire evidently thought it the best thing to do, and he hastily retreated without further words or ceremony.

Before the squire had time to cool down he met John, who was on his way to see Sara. Getting down from his horse, he shook his whip in the young man's face and inquired:

"Are you going to see that girl of Raguel's?"

John acknowledged that he was.

"Then," said the squire, "never darken my doors again. I will have all your belongings set right out in the yard before sundown."

John was slow to wrath, and as he looked on the purple, flushed face of his father, he knew that any more excitement might end in a serious illness, so he soothingly replied:

"All right, Father, I will go back home now with you."

His father had not counted on obedience to his wishes. His hands trembled so that he could scarcely hold the reins. John walked by the side of the horse and led the conversation away from all exciting subjects, and by the time they reached him the squire was outwardly calm. John left him and sat down beneath the old tree overhanging the garden, where he and Ruth always held tryst. In a few minutes the little girl joined him there, and her sharp eyes saw that something was wrong, and she inquired:

"What has happened now?"

John had been thinking it all over, and the situation appalled him. He was naturally of a quiet, complacent disposition. Anything like disturbance was intolerable to him. He wanted things to run smoothly along without much action on his part, but when something occurred to awaken him from his lethargy he was ready to act. That something had occurred now with a vengeance and he was compelled to face the problem and solve it.

Ruth's interruption recalled him from the pleasant musing that he was indulging in, for like a flash of lightning from out the sky had come the enlightenment of his senses. He knew that he loved Sara–that fact had been made clear to him. Why had he not known it sooner? What were all the misunderstandings, the wrath of his father or others, to him? What did he care for their bitterness of speech? He loved Sara. She was dearer than all else on earth to him. And these words came to his mind like an inspiration, "A man shall leave father and mother, cleaving only unto his wife." Surely that was clear enough. No man could have a grander possession than the heart of a pure woman, a pearl beyond great price.

The knowledge that had come to him quickened his desire to know if her love for him equaled that in his heart for her, and a great longing possessed him to go and tell to her all of his desires. Then over his dreams there crept a doubt that was torture. Perhaps she cared for him only as a good friend and comrade, and his longing to know the truth was overwhelming in its intensity.

Ruth had waited impatiently for an answer to her question, until Jack drew her down by his side:

"Little one," he said, "I am at my wits' ends. Not only has Father demanded that I marry the Lady Sophia, but some one has told him that I visit Sara. I met him coming from the direction of her father's house this afternoon, and he was in a towering rage. He told me that if I went there—and I had to tell him where I was going—that I need not come back home again. Now I suspect that he had been to the house, and I do not doubt that he said dreadful things. I came home with him to pacify and quiet him, for I was afraid that he might have a fit. I am sure, seeing the temper he was in, that he had given full rein to his speech and insulted Sara and her parents. She is expecting me, but I could not go and leave Father in such shape."

Ruth remained silent for a minute. Then she raised herself from the bench, and shaking down her tiny skirts and looking her brother straight in the eyes, she asked in a low, impressive voice:

"Jack, do you love Sara?"

Away in the distance one could see the farm hands swinging their scythes over the tall grass. Here and there one of the men stood apart sharpening the dull edges and preparing for another onslaught, while the tall utensils rested against walls or the gnarled trunk of an old tree. At their feet the insects fluttered about the tall grass, emitting little chirping sounds as they hopped. Down by the brook the cows were wading. Now and then a gentle mo-oo was wafted on the breeze: only the homely noises of the outlying farms—naught else to break the silence—a beautiful, peaceful scene that appealed to the heart and senses—and yet so at variance with the tumultuous moods of humanity! The heart of the man cried out for peace, and over his spirits a sadness fell, and he questioned, "Why should not all things be in keeping? Dear God, looking on this fleeting world, is there anything worth while? Shall we live and suffer grief, injustice, and bitterness of spirit, and all to what end?"

The young girl looked afar off over the hills at the western sky, and then again at her brother's face, where joy and sorrow blended, and a tender little tremor crept about the childish mouth, and out of the sad eyes there dawned a new light, the light of a woman's soul who saw and understood. She was stirred to the depths of her nature at this crisis, and in perfect sympathy with the man who felt that it was too late to turn back, and yet trembled to face all that was before him.

Ruth came to the rescue. She loved her big brother so well that she was able to put all selfish thoughts aside and think only of his happiness, and it seemed to her that it was best for him to have his heart's desire. Still she could not trust herself to break the silence.

He had looked at the childish face, and noted with wonder the transparent changes. At last he stood up, and from his greater height looked down on the quaint little figure. Then taking her close to his heart, he whispered:

"Dear little sister, yes, I love Sara with all my heart, but I am afraid that I can never claim her. I cannot see my way clear to anything. I don't know whether she loves me or not."

"Nonsense," broke in Ruth, coming suddenly down to earth again. "Of course she loves you. Any girl in her right senses must love you." And then with a determined expression she said: "The first thing to be done is for me to go straight over there and find out what Father said to them, and I am going at once. I can ride my pony, and no one need know anything about it except you and me. And you won't tell Father, will you?"—with a quizzical glance at him.

John did not know whether he ought to let her go or not. As she flitted away to get herself ready, he came to the conclusion that he would not be able to prevent her if he tried.

After Ruth left him, his mother came out to talk with him. These outdoor conferences had grown more frequent since there were guests in the house. She told him of the conversation she had with his father, and talked freely of her dislike towards the Lady Sophia, and it was a comfort to John to know that his mother did not second his father's wishes. She showed motherly compunction, however, in regard to Sara, saying:

"I wish that you had not set your heart on Raguel's daughter, as I suppose you have. I have never listened to the silly, wild stories that have been current about her, but the fact remains that all of her seven husbands have died almost directly after the marriage service has been performed. And I am afraid that only grief and sorrow can come if you persist in going there, and if you should marry her you will probably go the same way the rest have gone."

"Well now," said John, "who can say whether they all went the same way? Without joking, Mother, you know that it is foolish superstition and that I am not likely to die because they did. I have always been strong and well. Why should sudden death come to me? You surely are not so foolish as to believe that there is a curse resting on that innocent girl?"

"I don't know," said his mother helplessly. "I only wish that you had never seen her, and to think it is all your father's fault! And now to have him so set on your marrying that hateful Lady Sophia, whom I cannot abide. Oh dear, children are a great responsibility, and sometimes I wish that I had remained single. Then this thing never could have happened."

John smiled and said:

"Never mind, little Mother, it will all come right in the end—mark my words."

CHAPTER XIX

John Proposes Marriage to Sara

Meanwhile Ruth arrived at the farm, where her coming produced consternation. Sara was in her own room, where she had remained since the advent of the squire. Her father had told her the result of the interview.

"You hear what the squire said. John is promised to the Lady Sophia, and no one ever prospers if he breaks a promise. I hope, little girl, if you ever considered the young man as a suitor, you will try to put all such ideas out of your mind. You are of as good blood as the squire or any of his people, and we ask nothing of them."

Sara turned away without speaking. The squire's tirade had not disturbed her. The only words that hurt were, "John is promised to another." The sentence rang through her head until she was nearly crazed. Could it be true— John to belong to another? As she recalled the tender clasp of his hand, the little broken sentences that seemed to mean so much, the honest, true eyes, she said:

"If he is false, then naught is true. It is not true; I will not believe it." Yet Reason whispered, "What assurance have I that he loves me; what has he ever said? Only the indescribable language of love, without words." And then all of her native pride came to her aid and she said:

"I will tell him that he must do as his father commands, and then I will not see him alone again."

Cold and distant in manner, she came down to greet Ruth. The two had never been well acquainted. Sara was now twenty-three years of age, and Ruth so much younger than she that they had seldom met. John had told her so much that was good of the little girl that she had been prepared to like her until now, when her coming at this time seemed but another rebuke from the big house. Coldly her eyes questioned the young girl as she waited for her to make her business known. Ruth arose, as she always did when excited, and said:

"Oh, why do you make it so hard for me? I have not done anything to offend you! Why should you look at me in that cold, proud way?"

Then she put her head down on the table and sobbed aloud. Sara was surprised at her agitation and said to her:

"Do not cry, my dear; tell me, why have you sought me? Does your father know of your coming?"

"No, he doesn't," said Ruth. "If he had anything to say about it, I should be almost anywhere else." She wiped away her tears and continued:

"No one had better tell him that I have been here either, without they want their heads taken off from their shoulders. And yet, I have come on his account. I want you to tell me all about the row and what he said to you. Jack says that he knows that Father must have said terrible things, for he met him coming from here, and he was in an awful rage."

Sara became cold and reserved in her manner again, saying:

"I cannot tell you. You must ask your father what he said."

"Yes, don't you think it likely that I will thrust my head into the lion's jaws that way? Well, you don't need to tell me; knowing Father as I do, I can guess.

"You can be close-mouthed if you want to and not tell me anything. I will be more Christianlike and tell you something that you want to know, thought I must say you do not deserve it.

"Jack was on his way here to see you when he met Father, who was so mad that he fairly danced a jig, and he looked so purple in the face and fitty like that Jack expected every minute to see him tumble off from his horse. Jack said that he knew it would not do to excite him any further, so he quieted him the best he could and went back home with him.

"Some one has told him about Jack coming here to see you—purposely, we think, to make trouble, because Father has set his heart on having Jack marry the Lady Sophia Ainslie, and," with a toss of her head, "he will never get Jack to do it in the Lord's world, never! I know what I am talking about when I say that, too."

Sara blushed as Ruth looked questioningly at her, and she said:

"Your father told mine that John was promised to the young woman and that they were to be married soon."

"Promised your granny," said Ruth with a stamp of her foot "Well I vum! I knew Father was capable of almost anything when he is mad, but I did think he would draw the line at telling lies. And that is a whopper, the biggest one I ever heard.

"Jack never even liked the Lady Sophia, but I was so afraid that Father would browbeat him into paying some attention to her that I made him swear up and down on the Bible that he never would marry her, no matter what antics Father cut up. Not that he ever intended to marry her, but,"—with a wise little shake of the head—"you know what men are. And I was afraid that they might hoodwink him in some way. So that is settled, and if you will promise never to tell, I'll tell you something. "Jack is head over ears in love with you, and I guess that was what he was coming to tell you when all this powwow was kicked up."

The rosy pink blushes covered Sara's fair face, while teardrops glistened on the long eyelashes that rested against her delicate cheeks.

"Oh, how pretty you are," exclaimed Ruth impulsively. "No wonder Jack loves you," and she threw her arms about Sara's neck. The embrace was warmly returned, and the two became fast friends from that time on.

When Ruth arose to go she said:

"Jack wanted me to ask you to meet him down by the spring to-morrow. He thinks it will not be best for him to come here until after he has an understanding with Father."

Sara drew herself up proudly and looked hurt. Ruth smiled and said:

"Now don't be 'aughty, as Lady Sophia would say. You ought to know"— and she assumed great dignity—"that you can trust my brother Jack to do what is best and right."

After the exchange of a few more words Ruth went home. Sara had promised to be at the tryst the following day.

Raguel and Edna listened to the account Sara gave of Ruth's visit without comment. They both liked John, and Raguel made up his mind not to interfere, saying:

"The boy is his own master."

Sara was supremely happy and counting the hours that must elapse before the morrow afternoon. And as she went about the house, she sang a soft little air to herself. Her mother listened to the sweet voice, and from the depths of her heart a prayer ascended to God that happiness and good fortune might bless her child, and light from out the darkness be vouchsafed her.

When Ruth drew rein at her own door, at the back entrance, she found Jack awaiting her coming, and as he lifted her from the saddle, she looked smilingly at him and said:

"Be of good cheer, brother, for behold I bring you good tidings."

Jack cautioned her against acquiring the deacon's scriptural quotation habit.

When she had repeated all that there was to tell, he told her that he would never forget all that she had done to set this miserable business right. That his father told them what he did seemed incredible, and was proof that there was no telling to what lengths he would go to carry out his desires in this matter. John's pulses throbbed as his heart beat high with hope at the thought of meeting Sara on the morrow, for the hours had seemed long since they had been separated.

Ruth did not tell him of all the things she dis cussed with Sara. She deemed it wise to withold some of the information, knowing well that Sara would respect her confidence, and that nothing could keep John from saying all that was in his heart now that affairs had been brought to this climax.

Lady Sophia came out of the house at this juncture to join them. Ruth said it was a habit of Lady Sophia's to tag folks around.

The insipid talk of the woman had become dis tasteful to John, and he could not appear his natural self in her presence. Knowing his father's intentions regarding her, and suspecting her, that she had knowledge thereof, made him constrained and reserved in his manner towards her.

The atmosphere at the squire's house was getting rather cool, and with all Lady Sophia's conceit and obtuseness it was beginning to take effect. Ruth was barely civil, the squire's wife silent and abstracted, paying little heed to her conversation.

This day, affairs seemed to be a little worse than usual. She complained that night to her Aunt Charlotte that it was getting dull there, and that she was tired to death of that clodhopper John, who seems always to be looking at the ceiling and does not know how to behave in the presence of ladies.

"I think he treats me shamefully," said Lady Sophia, "and I shall go 'ome, and if Father wants the squire's money, 'e will 'arve to borrow it, and not go lowering me by throwing me at the 'ead of folks as is beneath me."

And having thus given vent to her feelings and, I am happy to say, proven that she was not quite the fool she had appeared to be, she shook out her flounces and looked sullen.

After supper, instead of remaining with the family until retiring time, as had been her custom, she excused herself and went to her room for the night. That left John free to go his own way, and the grass did not grow under his feet on his way to Raguel's house.

Sara met him in the doorway, and he clasped the slender hand in his own as the two walked through the hall to the best room where Raguel and Edna were. Sara tried to withdraw her hand, but John held it fast, and leading her to the chair where her father sat he said:

"Father Raguel, your daughter brings you a son. Am I acceptable in your sight? If so, give us your blessing."

Raguel smiled and said:

"What does the little girl say?"

Then Sara spoke up:

"Why, he has not asked my consent yet."

Raguel said:

"Sara must decide the question; if she is of the same mind as yourself, I will not withhold my consent."

When they were alone John told Sara that nothing could change his love for her, and as he was old enough to choose for himself, there was no reason why they should not marry at once, for her happiness and his own were to be the only considerations.

She acknowledged her love for him, and thought it would be well to wait for his father's consent before talking of marriage. She would like to put off the evil day as long as possible, for she was convinced that marriage with her meant death to the bridegroom, and she did not see why they could not remain as they were. She became excited over the subject, telling him that he was only courting death. He tried to calm her, and as she grew hysterical, he decided to let matters remain as they were for the present, with no talk of marriage.

John felt, now that he and Sara had come to an understanding, that the only honorable course was to inform his father of his intentions. Justice to Sara demanded this, for he was determined to visit her, and there were to be no clandestine relations between them. The next morning an opportunity came to speak with his father and he with directness announced his intentions, saying:

"I have been so fortunate as to win the heart of Raguel's daughter, and as soon as I can prevail upon her to set the day, we are to be married."

The squire answered him:

"The day that you marry that woman you cease to be son of mine. If you are so set upon going there to see her, I suppose that you will go, as you are of age and your own master, but the day she appoints for the wedding I will instruct the sexton to dig a grave for you in the family plot in the churchyard, and that is the last thing I shall do. I will not countenance your doings by going to your funeral, and let me tell you this, young man: you are as good as dead now in the eyes of all the neighborhood—for the end is not far off."

John felt that it would not be wise to have any more words on the subject. He had accomplished his end, and was thankful that the squire had taken his announcement as calmly as he had done.

Later on be repeated the result to Ruth, and she comforted him, saying:

"Dad is surely breaking down, and all will come right in the end." And with merry cheerfulness she made light of her father's words.

As soon as she had an opportunity, she told the Lady Sophia that Jack was engaged to be married to the sweetest, handsomest girl in the world, and that she and her mother were delighted over it. Lady Sophia concluded that was the key to his indifference to her own charms, and consoled herself by thinking that the girl was probably of his own station and, no doubt, better fitted to be his wife—and having thus digested the news, hastened her preparations for departure.

The squire attended her to the city, and by his gallant attentions and courtesy tried to cover up his chagrin over the way the visit had terminated. Like the wise man that he was, he kept his own counsel, but his antipathy towards Sara increased in volume, and he treated his son with contemptuous silence.

CHAPTER XX

The Indian Woman

The Indian wigwams had been raised in the fields for a number of months, and the Indians were all about in their old haunts.

Raguel had cautioned Sara against taking her accustomed long walks over hill and dale. Although the tribe appeared friendly, it was wise to give them a wide berth.

Several days had elapsed now since word had been received that the wigwams had been abandoned and the Indians had moved on, and Sara was ready for a long walk, with the sense of freedom that comes when any restraint has been lifted. She had walked only a few rods in the woods when she heard a peculiar noise like the sound of one moaning in pain. She stood still and listened, trying to locate the sound. At times it was so weak that she thought it might be a bird that had been injured. She followed the path in the direction of the sound. As she went on it became louder and clearer—evidently a human being in distress.

Out in the open field she made the discovery. An aged Indian woman lay there on the ground, an old blanket beneath her. Scattered about on the ground were fragments of food. There was nothing to protect her from the elements, and she seemed to be nearly dead. Sara spoke to her and she opened her eyes in a dazed way and looked at her, then closed them again.

It was difficult to know what was best to do. Sara knew enough about Indian habits to be sure that the woman had been abandoned by them on account of her infirmities, and had been left to die alone, as was their custom when one of their number became so old or so ill as to be a helpless burden.

Sara went out to the highway and called to some laborers in an adjoining field. They came and looked at the old woman and refused to lend any aid in removing her, saying:

"She is no good. Let her die. She's most dead anyhow. It is like warming a rattlesnake to have anything to do with Injuns."

There was no other resource for Sara but to go home and find her father or one of the farm hands. It was not humane to leave her there. Fortunately, Raguel was at home, and he called two of his men to assist him. They fixed some bedding and blankets in an oxcart and went after her. Raguel said:

"Another night's exposure would probably kill her. The clouds look like rain, and the poor old creature would be drowned before to-morrow morning. I am not sure but that it would be the best thing that could happen to her. I suppose if we take her in and she lives, the first thing she does, most likely, will be to pizen some of us, but there don't seem to be anything else to be done. We shall have to take the risk. She will die most likely, and I wouldn't leave a beast to die in that inhuman way."

So the old Indian was carried to the farmhouse. A room was fixed up for her in one of the outhouses, where she was made comfortable and nursed back to health and strength, for there was a large amount of vitality in the old body, and it was probable that she would live many years longer now that she had had proper care and nourishment. As she grew better, she watched all that was done for her with sharp eyes that looked out of a stolid, inscrutable countenance.

Sara frequently attended to her needs, and at such times there was a degree of interest in the glittering eyes, and she turned her head to watch each movement of the graceful figure, while she grunted several times in a manner that seemed to betoken her gratification, although the sound could in no wise be confounded with words.

One morning Sara went out to the building to carry her the broth that she had prepared for her. She found her standing erect, and with one hand pointing towards the east, she commenced speaking:

"Before many moons I shall join my people. I also am named Sara by my father, who was a missionary. He taught me many words of the white man's language. My mother was an Indian maiden whose people belonged to one of the Ten Lost Tribes of Israel. My father and mother have long since entered the spirit land.

"The Great Spirit instructed the white maiden to succor me. The white man has given me his hospitality. I have my strength again. The Great Spirit has raised me up that I may gain a victory over the evil spirit that has so long vexed the White Lily, and destroy his power to harm the White Lily and her race. I go forth. Eight times will the sun rise and set, and I come not. But on the ninth day, at the rising of the sun, will I come again. And at my coming a brilliant sun shall rise for the White Lily. Farewell."

And she stalked forth.

When Sara told her father that the woman had gone and of the words she had spoken, he smiled and said:

"That is Indian, hifalutin' talk. We have seen the last of her, and a good riddance."

John and Ruth were frequent visitors at the farm. The squire had forbidden Ruth to go there, but she openly defied him, and as she met with no opposition from her mother, he found it useless trying to enforce his commands. Mrs. Mildrum said to the squire:

"You have humored her and allowed her to have her own way all of her life, and it is rather late in the day to try to change things now."

And the squire had about come to the same conclusion. He had met Ruth one morning just as she was turning into the lane that led to the farmhouse, and he sternly commanded her to go back home. She retorted:

"Now, Dad, you can't boss me. I'm too old and know my own mind too well."

And kissing her hand, she wafted a kiss towards him, nimbly skipping over the ground until she disappeared in the house before he realized that she was going to defy him.

Sara enjoyed Ruth's companionship. Always bright and merry, she did much towards keeping Sara cheerful and happy. Raguel and Edna made a pet of the girl. Her witty sayings were a perfect delight to them, and she was as much at home among them as Sara was.

John's affection for Sara increased with association, but whenever he spoke of marriage he found her implacable. She always replied:

"Let the evil day remain afar off."

And he was obliged to acquiesce. But he continued his attentions and cultivated patience, trusting that the time would come when his faithfulness would gain its reward.

CHAPTER XXI

Tobit's Lost Son

A wide plain in a western village where the early autumn sun beat down its hot rays on the white sand. By the side of a winding river along the glittering sand came the tall figure of a man, walking slowly and hesitatingly with the pitifully sad movements of the blind. A tiny black and tan dog ran beside him, sometimes rushing along to the front, again close at his heels, and never ceasing in his watchful care—with little snappy barks and growls answering the words that the man addressed to him. As he drew too near the water the little dog caught hold of his breeches and frantically tried to hold him back. The man stepped backward, saying:

"Yes, yes, Rex, good doggie, I'll not get my feet wet. I will just drop down on the sand and you run and see if the Missus is coming."

A patter of swift dog feet and a sharp, glad bark in dog language told the recumbent man that the little dog had found what he sought. In a moment the man's trained ear caught the rustling sound of starched petticoats, and then a complaining voice reached him:

"It's a mercy that you are not drowned, Tobit, and I am thinking that the time will come when they will bring you home to me a stiff corpse, with all the starch rung out of your shirt front that I takes as much pains with as ever was to have it look even better than the parson's do on a Sunday. The little dog is all that keeps you from death, and I'm allus fearsome that he will be looking after a bone some 'ots when he should be watching you, and that will be the last of you."

"Now, Anna, say no more. Rex knows his duty too well to let harm come to the old man. I felt as if I must wander by the river this day, for my heart is heavy and sad, and the low murmur of the river comforts and soothes me. If my son had been spared to us, this would have been his thirtieth birthday."

"And do I not know it!" replied Anna. "When his mother forgets, then indeed would all things become strange. But how did you know it, Tobit? I have thought of naught else for the past week, but I said 'I will not add to his father's grief by mentioning it.'"

Tobit answered:

"I heard parson say yesterday that it was very warm for the first day of September, and so of course I knew when the sun rose this morning that it was the second day of the month. And why, will you tell me, woman," his voice rising in his excitement, "should those red devils have stolen my only son? And if it was for a ransom, as some folks have said, why were we not so informed, and why was the birth record stolen?"

"There, there, Father, I don't know. No one knows, and don't you go for exciting yourself and getting all worked up, as you know is very bad for you. I'm sure," she added in a complaining voice, "that it is bad also for me, his mother who bore him, to go down to her grave with no knowledge of where or when his little life ended, or whether he was tortured and abused, or whether he is living to-day reared by savages, and taught all their wicked, heathenish ways.

"Sometimes the horror of thinking that he may come home with feathers in his hair and dressed in animal skins strikes an awful sickness all over me. And I think," lowering her voice, "if it has pleased God to take him to Himself in his innocent babyhood I should be grateful and glad, but how are we ever to know until Judgment Day?

"But, dear heart, you must not look so sad and down-hearted. There may be some good in store for you yet, and we must remember what parson read from the Good Book only last Sunday, 'God loveth whom He chasteneth.' Though I can't help thinking it is a strange way to be a-showing of His love. I could understand His restoring your eyesight, and sending my baby back to me again, but alas, this is not the age of miracles, and we can only wait His time.

"And to think no other child of our blood has ever been born, and no other little one has ever rested in the cradle we had made for him. I think the reason is because of my fretting so uncommon-like for him as the Injuns stole.

"And to think if he were alive he might be living on his own estate, and lording it in old England at the castle that his uncle willed to him as next of kin, and his heart set on having it so. And now his cousin Sophia is there instead, and as stuck up and hateful a thing as ever was.

"I am thinking Tobias would never have been willing to marry such a girl of bad disposition, but the property would have been his just the same. His uncle looked out for all that. The lad was to please himself about the marriage, and I must say he treated him fair—as if he were his own son, as he wished it to appear."

As they drew near their home, a slender man of medium height, dressed in a neat black suit, came hurriedly down the walk to meet them. The woman held her husband's hand in her own, tightly clasped. She withdrew her hand and stopped in amazement, saying:

"I think that is the parson coming to meet us. Some'at must have happened surely. Oh, whatever new trouble has come upon us."

The clergyman stopped, as they had done, in the middle of the walk, and said:

"My friends, I have important news for you."

And as he noticed their increased agitation, he hastened to say:

"There is a clew to your long-lost son's disappearance. One of the squaws belonging to the Pawtucket tribe in the East has come here with a strange story. She is very old, and has recently been converted to our religion by a missionary who has done good work among the different tribes here in the West.

"She says that since she has learned right from wrong she could not rest until she had told all that she knew concerning the cruel wrong perpetrated thirty years ago, when one of the Indians stole your son from his cradle with the intention of rearing him as a great medicine man, and because no son of his own had been born to him. I infer, judging from her talk, that underneath all that there was a motive. No doubt but that it was revenge."

"Yes," said Anna. "I have always thought that. I know Tobit made enemies of them, though I never dared to say it before, fearing to add to his burden.

"It was like this. We were tormented by their thieving, and Tobit had a young Injun locked up for breaking into our granary. I have often thought that it would have been better to have let the meal go and said nothing, but Tobit was hot-headed those days, and would have it that something must be done to stop them from stealing."

"Your son was stolen," continued the parson, "by one of the tribes belonging to the East. The child's face was stained and he was wrapped in skins and kept out of sight as much as possible, until there was no longer danger of pursuit.

"One evening a white woman came to the camp. Underneath her shawl she carried a dead infant. The child looked to be about ten days old.

"The woman explained that she was a nurse and that, as she was preparing the child for bed, she accidently dropped it on the stone hearth. The little one only breathed a few gasping breaths after she raised it in her arms, and then it straightened out its little limbs and ceased to breathe. She had been too frightened to give any alarm and, obeying her first impulse, had wrapped it in a blanket and left the house with it. There were no definite plans for disposing of it in her mind at the time–only the fear and horror of what would be done when the child's death was discovered and she would be accused of murder. Instinctively she walked towards the woods as the best place for disposing of her burden. And as she drew near the Indian camp, the thought came to her that she could probably hire one of them to bury the body for her.

"Before she had left the house she had caught up her purse and a small leather bag that contained a few pieces of jewelry. The Indians were loath to take the dead child, but she brought forth the ornaments, and with a few dollars thrown in, she prevailed upon one of them to do her bidding.

"She had noticed while talking with the Indian that there seemed to be a controversy between several of them at a short distance from where she stood.

"As she started to leave the woods, an old squaw came towards her with a living child in her arms. She stopped to look at the baby. The woman came forward and offered to give it to her to take the place of the dead infant.

"The nurse closely examined the child, and behold, it was an exact counterpart of the dead body. The child was of white parentage, although its face had been stained. It was of the male sex and might have been the twin of the other one, with the exception that the living child was probably several weeks the elder.

"The Indians expressed themselves as glad to get rid of the child without explaining how it had come into their possession. Evidently it had become a burden to them through fear of detection and its consequences, and it was a bother to be always disguising and watching over it. So the exchange was made, the Indian promising to carry out his part of the compact in burying the child.

"The nurse joyfully returned to the home of her employers, and without compunction substituted the living child. The plan was entirely successful. She had returned as quickly and secretly as possible and entered the house and nursery unseen, and in a short period had the child in a warm bath. The squaw had given her a wash for removing the stain from the baby's skin, and after he had par taken of a bottle of warm milk and been dressed in the little garments so daintily fashioned for the little son of the house, all was in readiness to carry out the design of the nurse.

"There was small danger of detection. The mother had been at the point of death and was not yet out of danger. The room was kept darkened. She had been too sick to get a very distinct idea of how the baby looked. The father was so distressed over the condition of his wife and, fearing that she would not recover, had paid little attention to the child. The day it was born he had taken it in his arms a minute and then laid it down by the side of the girl-mother. A few hours later she had become delirious, and her condition had given him great anxiety ever since.

"The nurse had been given full charge of baby, and thus it was made possible for the little stranger to usurp the place of the dead baby and grow up in the home that he had no legal right to. Innocent of any wrong, and with no knowledge of his rightful parentage, he had grown to manhood, loved and cherished by the fond mother and father who never had the slightest suspicion that he was not of their own flesh and blood."

CHAPTER XXII

THE INDIAN WOMAN RETURNS

On the ninth day the Indian woman returned to the house of Raguel, as she had said she would do, and beckoning Sara to follow, she led the way to the building that had been her shelter when Raguel had brought her from the woods more dead than alive. She motioned Sara to a seat on one of the rough benches, and towering above her said:

"The White Lily must marry the young white chief who has won her heart.

"Following the traditions of my tribe, I have brought the heart and liver and the gall of a fish. If a devil or evil spirit trouble any we must make a smoke thereof before the man or woman, and the party shall be no more vexed. As for the gall, it is good to anoint a man that has whiteness in his eyes, and he shall be healed.[2]

And suiting the action to the word, she made a smoke of the heart and the liver and gall before Sara, and therewith solemnly declared that the evil spirit had fled. Then she gave to Sara the remains of the gall in ashes, saying:

"Take care of this until the day it is needed."

"The lowering clouds are disappearing and a brilliant sun shall shine on the White Lily and the young chief, who shall be returned to his own people, and there will be great rejoicing. Hasten the marriage feast, and fear not. We shall meet again." And turning abruptly, she walked swiftly away.

The squaw's words made a strong impression on Sara, and she quickly sought her father and communicated what the Indian woman had said and done. Raguel pondered long on the subject and questioned Sara regarding all details of the woman's language and behavior. Then he said:

"I never expected to see or hear from her again, but I am compelled to believe that she has spoken with wisdom and understanding and I think, daughter, that you had better follow her teachings. We will consult your mother and John, and if they are of our mind we will prepare for the marriage."

---

[2] Tobit, Chapter VI, Apocrypha.

"But what is the meaning of her words regarding John's return unto his people?"

"Perhaps she means that his father will become reconciled to the marriage."

When John came he listened gravely to all that the squaw had said. Then, taking Sara by the hand, he led her to her father, saying:

"Father, give us your blessing. The marriage cannot be consummated any too soon to suit my wishes," and affectionately kissing Sara, he added, "I love and honor her above all women, and will be a good husband to her and a son to you and her mother."

So the preparations for the wedding began and all was cheerful in the house of Raguel.

The squire was told that the day had been set for the wedding and the fit of rage that convulsed him nearly ended his life. The prompt action of the doctor with lancet and leeches was all that saved him. The doctor warned him that another exhibition of the same kind would probably produce apoplexy and paralysis. That admonition restrained him for a few days, but with returning strength the strong self-will grew dominant again, and the day he was able to leave his room found him superintending the removal of John's effects from the house. He had ordered them all put out in the yard, and when John arrived on the scene he informed him that he was not going to harbor such an ingrate as he was any longer.

There was a terrible scene between the squire and his wife, but John quieted and soothed her.

"It is only a few days ahead of time," he said, "for I should be gone next week anyway. When I have a home of my own it will always be open to you, my dear mother."

These were troublous days for the poor mother who almost idolized her stalwart son. There was little sympathy between the squire and his wife. She had always been gentle and submissive, while he was domineering and ugly-tempered, seldom speaking a pleasant word in the house, taciturn and sullen in disposition, until some trifling thing gave him opportunity to display his temper. Then every one who could fled before it. No one but Ruth ever dared to answer back or contradict him, no matter how unreasonable he was. She would not tolerate his sarcastic speeches, always turning on him and in the end holding him up to ridicule.

"Poor mammy," she would say to her mother, "if I could take your place I would soon make a different man of him."

Shortly after the squire's interview with John he blustered into the room where Ruth and her mother were holding converse, and looking at Ruth, while the pale wife sat down all of a tremble, like a leaf in the wind, he said:

"Now, daughter, after this day you are not going to have anything to do with that scapegoat of a brother."

"Who said so?" answered Ruth.

"I say so. As he has made his bed, so shall he lie. I'll not have his goings-on upheld by any member of this household and," glaring at his wife, "no whimpering or pleading will make any difference to me. I have discarded him forever—though the Lord knows I believe that his days are numbered and his end not far off, if he is cut down as the rest of that girl's bridegrooms have been and there's no reason to suppose that he will be spared; and it will be just punishment for his disobedience."

Ruth got the camphor for her mother, who was on the verge of fainting. Then, as her father continued his harangue, Ruth's temper began to rise, and as he ended his talk with: "If ever you step foot in Raguel's house, or speak to your brother or that Sara, you are no daughter of mine, and you will go out of my house in the same way that your brother has gone."—Ruth faced him, and in spite of her mother's imploring looks, she marched up to him. Shaking her little fist in his face, she said:

"You miserable contemptible old coward, you! You are no father of mine; I disown you. You browbeat and make poor Mother tremble in her shoes, but you cannot scare me. I despise you for your ugly, hateful words to my mother and good brother Jack. I don't care a copper for what you say to me, and I want you to know that I'll not only set my foot in Sara's house, but I'll get there with both feet. And when I get ready to come home here I shall come, and I should just like to see you or any other old daddy keep me out of my own home. So you can put that in your pipe and smoke it."

By this time her fury had spent itself, and Ruth looked in her father's face and smiled. He turned from her and walked out of the room with the knowledge that, in spite of Ruth's smiles, she would defy him and go her own sweet way, and he chucked to himself at the thought of her shaking her fist at him, and said:

"The girl has my grit, but the boy is like his mother and will not fight."

John had his clothing and other effects removed to Raguel's house. Raguel and Edna made him welcome, saying:

"The wedding is not far off and you are in all respects our son."

As one might expect, the neighbors talked, and many of them took sides with the squire, while others said that John had done right, and as any young man of age and knowing his own mind should have done, and the latter outnumbered the former, for the squire was not a popular man. Too many of his neighbors had found him a hard, unyielding man in his dealings—a man who always had the best end of a bargain, no matter who suffered on account of it.

As soon as possible Ruth got ready to visit Sara. Her father watched her movements, and when she went to her room he followed her and saw, as he had suspected, that she was putting on her outdoor garments. He remained in the hall until she came out ready to go, then he inquired:

"Where are you going?"

And Ruth answered flippantly:

"Why don't you say the rest? Where are you going, my pretty maid? And if you must know, I am going to see my sister-in-law that is to be."

"By the living prophets you shall not!" said the squire. "I'll see if I am to be defied in my own house. I will tie you to the bedpost first."

And he caught the frail figure in his arms and thrust her into the chamber again. Ruth was startled, for her father had always been gentle in his treatment towards her, with the exception of sharp speeches, without trying to enforce his commands.

She sat down on the bed, and tears of mortification and anger rolled down her face, but she grieved only a short time. The indignant blood surged in her cheeks. Drying her eyes, she stepped to the door, but she tried in vain to open it, and she knew by the sound of movements on the other side that her father was holding it fast.

She went to the other side of the room and her eyes sought the open window. The branches of a large cherry tree held her attention. Then a smile broke through the clouds, and softly pushing the window frame up higher— as far as it would go—she surveyed the tree and, catching her tiny skirts in her hand, she jumped and crashed among the leaves; grasping the branches above her with both hands, she swung herself to a crotch of the tree. She wrapped one hand in her handkerchief and, holding on to the different boughs, she scrambled as best she could to the ground in safety, although the skin on one small hand was torn and bleeding, and the shock to the delicate system was great. If she had been straight in figure, with the strength and practice that other girls of her age living in the country generally have, she probably would not have been any the worse for it. Her affliction made her weak and her limbs had not been strengthened by the merry romps that other children enjoyed. As soon as she could get her breath she hastened down the walk, looking nervously about. As the coast seemed to be clear, she left the yard and hurried down the road.

Her mother had waited at the foot of the stairs, expecting she did not know what, but fearing a terrible outbreak of some kind, for she thought the squire was acting like a crazy loon.

He held on to the door for several minutes and, because he heard no sound from the room, his curiosity got the better of him and he cautiously opened the door, expecting to see the childish form. Astonished at not seeing her, but suspecting some trick, he closed the door and proceeded to investigate, going cautiously to each nook and corner. Then, as he saw the open window and the broken branches of the tree, his hard old heart nearly stopped beating as an awful fear took possession of him, and for a moment he was bereft of power to move, and he dared not look on the ground beneath the tree.

At the first discovery he had given an involuntary cry of alarm. His wife heard and hurried up the stairs. When she entered the room and saw his agitated countenance, the strain was too much for her weak nerves and she screamed:

"What have you done? Have you killed her?"

She saw that Ruth was gone, and in her anxiety for her child she lost all fear of the squire.

"Answer me," she demanded, "you heartless man, and then get out of my sight before I forget God's teachings and kill you. You were not satisfied with depriving me of my son, and now you have sent my little crippled daughter to her death."

The old man for once could make no reply, but sat with bowed head and trembling mien, and it was the mother who looked and leaned far out of the window to scan the ground beneath the tree, expecting to see the crushed and bleeding form. A few dry branches and curling leaves lay on the ground, and that was all she could see, until she raised her eyes to the distant roadway just in time to see a small figure fast vanishing in the turn of the road. She said not a word, but went quickly from the room and down the stairs, meekly followed by the squire who asked:

"Did you see anything out there?"

She made no answer, and the squire went out and examined the ground under the tree. Then he said:

"It looks as if she might have fallen here. Do you suppose she hurt herself? And have you any idea where she is? I think perhaps she is hiding somewheres round."

The woman looked coldly at him and did not answer.

Ruth was his idol, and the long hours of the day dragged wearily away. In the afternoon his wife appeared before him in her bonnet and mantle and said:

"I am going to Raguel's house to inquire about Ruth."

And the squire made no protest, and it is probable that he realized that it would not have made any difference if he had. The reins of government seemed to have been taken entirely out of his hands and he guessed that it was pretty nearly time for the world to come to an end.

Mrs. Mildrum found Ruth in bed. Edna had thought of sending for her at once, but Ruth made such a fuss that she concluded to wait until towards night and then send word to the squire's house without consulting Ruth. Her mother saw that she ought to have advice, and sent at once for the doctor. The girl appeared very ill, the pain in her back was bad, and the shock and excitement had brought on a nervous chill. The doctor came and said that she must be kept quiet in bed for a few days. She had strained some of the muscles and was badly shaken up.

Her mother remained with her until evening. When she reached home the squire came to meet her. When he found that Ruth was not likely to die, he began to rave and storm in his usual way. Bringing his fist down on the table so that the dishes danced a jig, he shouted:

"She shall be brought home this very night. We shall see who is master here."

A dignified, sorrowful woman faced him, saying:

"Hush your tirade. The child is mine as well as yours, and *I* say that she shall not be disturbed. No, not if I have to call on the authorities to restrain you." And that ended the discussion.

The house was quiet and strange and the squire had ample time to miss his children. There were no outbreaks on his part, but he looked fretful and sullen.

It was a full week before Ruth was able to be about the house. Her mother had taken her necessary clothing to her, and a new frock was in progress of completion that greatly interested her, for she was to wear it at the wedding.

Ruth was not usually vindictive, but she expressed herself as having no desire to see her father. She said:

"I am tired of him and I don't mean to go home at present."

Her mother brought messages from her father, begging her to come home. Ruth had laid down certain rules to him, and unless he complied with them she would not agree to go. He was willing to make all sorts of concessions so far as she was concerned, but he continued to utterly disown John.

At last Ruth decided to go home. Her father took her in his arms, and when she saw his agitation and the excitement he was under she gave up all thought of the scolding that she had made up her mind to administer to him. His trembling hands and tearful eyes appealed to the girl's tender heart, and she clasped her arms about his neck and gave him a hug and a kiss, saying:

"Dear old Dad, you just let me have my own way—you know it is a good way—and everything will be all right."

Her father looked at the bright happy face, and with a contented sigh resigned himself to another bug. No more words were necessary. The squire knew that Ruth had won and that he had been vanquished.

CHAPTER XXIII

THE EIGHTH MARRIAGE

For the eighth time Sara was to be given in marriage. It was a gala day in the village, for those who were not invited to the feast were under the excitement of the hour.

The squire had gone to the sexton and ordered him to prepare a grave for John in the family plot in the graveyard. He was fully persuaded—or pretended to be (and one cannot deny that there was reason) that John would die on his wedding day.

The old sexton was in sympathy with the squire, and thought it well to have the grave in readiness. There was not much doubt but that it would be needed in a few hours. But until the young man died it did not appear seemly to dig the grave, and he refused to do it.

The squire, not to be outwitted, waited until a late hour that night and, taking the necessary implements, with the aid of two workingmen the grave was speedily opened.

Shortly after sunrise an awe-struck crowd of spectators had assembled near the graveyard, and with curious glances and whispered words pointed out to each newcomer the open grave.

Only a few intimate friends and relatives were bidden to the wedding. Julia's husband, the Rev. James White, would officiate. Julia had been very kind and sisterly towards Sara, and the happiest relations were sustained between them.

If there were trepidation and fear expressed by the neighbors that this marriage would end in grief and sorrow, as the preceding ones had done, no such fear affected the contracting parties.

All were happy and joyful at Raguel's house. Edna had laid aside all fear, and looked younger and more joyous than she had since the early days of her own marriage, for she believed implicitly all of the words spoken by the Indian woman. The burning of the fish's heart, liver and gall was looked upon by them all as a sacred rite that destroyed the power of the evil spirit to work any more harm.

Ruth had recovered her health and spirits and had come with her mother to help array Sara in her bridal robes. She had heard of the open grave, and laughed at her father as she told him that "she thought he would feel pretty small at the little end of the horn when he saw the lively corpse Jack would be the day after the wedding."

Abby Ann Eaton was on hand, and for over a week she had been putting forth her best efforts in the culinary line, contributing the best of everything that would make Sara's wedding feast something that should be talked of for years to come.

The deacon would not be present at the wedding, and Abby Ann "allowed that he had been particularly aggravating that morning, hindering her in every possible way."

For one thing he had made an unusually long prayer, stretching it out and saying the same things over and over again until she called a halt, being unable to stand the strain any longer, with all the day's work before her and not a moment to spare. She called out:

"Come, deacon, for pity's sake say Amen! I feel like firing something at your head. If the Lord is as tired of hearing that old yarn as I am He quit listening long ago, and you may as well git up off your knees and go about your business." And she rattled the dishes so loud that it drowned the sound of his voice.

When Abby Ann had announced her intention to help out on the cooking for Sara's wedding, the deacon forbade her to do anything of the kind. She paid not the slightest attention to him, but went quickly about doing what she thought was best. He got scared when she gave an extra order for groceries at the store, and made another attempt to stop proceedings. Then Abby Ann "took the question by the horns, so to speak, and settled it for good and all," saying:

"I am too old to expect children of my own. I love Sara as if she were my own daughter, and all that I am going to do for her is a labor of love, and no one is going to cheat me out of it. She shall have the best that I can do for her."

And Abby Ann's best was very near perfection, and it was owing to her good offices that Sara had the grandest wedding dinner that had ever been given in Kensington. She also prepared table and bed linen of the finest. When it was bleached and ready she brought it to Edna for inspection, saying:

"Our little gal shall have the best settin' out that any one in this village has ever seen."

It was a May day wedding, warm enough for the windows to be open, and the perfume of the spring flowers wafted in. The young couple were well mated and fair to look upon—she in her calm, sweet loveliness, he in his manly strength, with the stamp of nobility and frank honesty in every feature.

They were married in the front room of the old farmhouse where Sara had first opened her eyes to the light of day.

Her father said afterward that "for the life of him he could not keep from thinking of the day that the old wooden cradle had stood right there by the fireplace where Sara stood now a bride." And he seemed to see again the baby face and wonderful blue eyes looking up at him from out the white blankets that enveloped the baby form.

Now his little daughter with the crown of woman hood upon her brow raised the same truthful blue eyes to receive the tender glance of her husband. And Raguel, beholding them thus, felt that all that had gone before had vanished with the past like darkest night, and out of anguish and despair had come new light and life. For he was imbued with faith and trust, believing in the Indian woman's words that the curse had been lifted.

It was a happy wedding. As the ceremony ended, a low murmur of voices came from the yard in the front of the house, and a strange sight met the astonished eyes of the wedding guests. Out on the wide plot of green lawn a number of Indians sat, smoking the calumet of peace. As they looked, one of the red men arose and motioned the rest to follow in his footsteps.

He stopped at John's side and handed him a parcel wrapped in birch-bark from the white birch tree. The inner wrappers were of skin. From beneath several wrappings John drew forth a Bible leaf containing a birth record. There had been several names written at the top of the page. The last entry read, "Tobias, the son of Tobit of the tribe of Nephthalia."

When John read the names aloud the Indians gave a grunt of approval. When he repeated the last name the Indian who had presented the parcel stepped forward and placed his hand on John's breast, and said:

"You, Tobias—arise and go to your people." Then he took from the wrappings another piece of bark and pointed to the written name of a western town.

As he moved aside, the other Indians filed by one by one and deposited gifts at Sara's feet. There were a variety of ornaments made from bark and headed work, moccasins beautifully embroidered, and many useful as well as ornamental gifts, wooden porringers and dishes of quaint design, and elegant basketwork. After depositing their gifts they filed out as silently as they had entered. The old squaw, whom Sara had nursed back to health, was the last to take leave. Her parting words were:

"The Great Spirit watches over the White Lily. Fear no evil, for all is well."

The Indian's words and the birth record were unintelligible to John and were discussed with much speculation, but no one could fathom the mystery, and John concluded that the only thing to do was to wait for further instruction.

All joined merrily in the wedding feast, and the festivities were continued until a late hour. Ample justice was done to Abby Ann's cooking and many compliments were paid to her skill. At last the guests who had come from a distance retired to their rooms, and the house grew quiet.

The upper front chamber had been prepared for the bridal couple, and Ruth had the arrangement of it, and under her active hands it became a per feet bower of flowers.

In a few hours the house was all astir again. The bright spring sunshine shone in at the open casement, and the birds were holding a morning concert in the orchard.

All of the family had assembled in the wide room where the tables had been set the night before. The breakfast was a scene of jollity, and if there were any anxious fears regarding the bridegroom's welfare they were quickly allayed, for he appeared among them in his usual good health, while Sara assisted her mother in preparing breakfast for the company.

Raguel had arisen at five o'clock, as was his custom, to superintend the morning's work. The late hour of retiring made no difference with him or Edna, for there was work to be done, and every one in that household had duties and expected to attend to them.

Raguel went out to the garden, and his gaze wandered away to the hills and then to the green sward of the meadows. A startled exclamation from him brought Edna to his side. He pointed to a short distance away towards the east where an Indian but had been erected.

"Now," said Raguel, "why have those fellows camped down there? Something is to pay as sure as you live. Well, we shall know before nightfall, and I guess it concerns us or they would not have camped here on my land. There is more to be told, I am thinking."

The Indians had raised their wigwam with the intention of waiting there patiently until the messenger they had sent returned from an Illinois town.

Before breakfast was served at the farmhouse Raguel knelt by his chair, and each head was reverently bowed while he prayed a prayer of thankfulness and rejoicing that the curse that had for so long a time rested upon them had been lifted, and that out of much sorrow and tribulation had come joy and peace.

The word had gone forth throughout the village "that all was well at Raguel's house," and before noon many friends hastened there to extend congratulations and express good wishes for continued happiness and prosperity.

Ruth and her mother were in the breakfast room when Sara and John came down from the upper chamber, and after Ruth had given each an ecstatic hug, she said:

"I am going home to tell Father that the best thing he can do with that grave is to jump into it, for I guess he will want to hide his head somewhere."

The grave had been attended to by the young men of the village, friends of John, who filled the dirt back into it and tried to remove all signs of the broken earth.

The digging of the grave had caused a great scandal. Many people thought that the authorities ought to take some action and punish the perpetrator of such desecration. Deacon Eaton said:

"The squire ought sartainly to he took up for doing sech a thing, and if it had been enybody but old Squire Mildrum, he would ha' bin, and sent to jail, too." And when nothing was done about it, he told Abby Ann "that it seemed as if some folks thought that if they had a leetle money that they could do anything and not git teched for it."

CHAPTER XXIV

Tobit's Son Restored to Him

At sundown the Indians filed up to the house again. The squaw who had made the journey to the west came forward, and the chief with a grunt of disapproval pushed her aside, and with many gestures and forcible language he told the story of the kidnapping of a baby from its western home. He produced a letter from a clergyman of the town, Parson Woolly, who had done all that he could towards righting the wrong. The letter gave a full account of the story as the Indian squaw had told it to Parson Woolly.

The Indian waited in dignified silence while John read the letter aloud. It seemed incredible to him, for if the story therein was true, then he was the son of parents living in Illinois, and the squire and his wife whom he had always claimed as father and mother were no relation to him. He read and re-read the letter and the birth record. Then he announced his intention to go to the squire, and with the proofs in his hands tell him the story.

What a strange story it was! And what would the squire say when he told him that he was not of his blood? How entirely impossible the whole thing seemed! And he went to the home of his childhood and youth to talk with the man he had always looked upon as father.

Strange thoughts surged through his mind, and for the first time in his life he allowed the feeling that had always been dominant to reign—the feeling of repulsion towards the squire. He had fought against it all of his life, for his heart had never owned allegiance to the man whom he had been taught to call father. The mother was dear to him, and he would always retain the tenderest affection for her who seemed a part of his existence.

His mind was in a turmoil. But rising out of the labyrinth of questionings and surprise at the situation came the exultant thought–"That man is not my father; I am not of his flesh and blood." He could not at this time feel even the natural thankfulness that he should for the benefits of a good home and the education and care that he had received.

When John reached the house he hesitated about entering. The excitement of the discovery had been so great and his desire to at once acquaint the squire with the story had driven from his mind the squire's command that he was never to enter the house again. As his footsteps faltered, the squire, who had seen him coming, came out of the house and shouted:

"What are you doing here on my premises, young man? Do you want me to set the dog on you?"

John smiled at the idea of setting old Carlo to drive him away. The old dog was devoted to John and, hearing the loud voice of the squire, he had rushed round from the side of the house. When he saw John he wagged his tail in satisfaction and then, growing more demonstrative, gave a loud bark of welcome, placing his forefeet on John's shoulder to further emphasize his greeting. John shook the old fellow's paw, and at this juncture Ruth and her mother came out of the house.

The squire demanded again to know why he had come, saying:

"You are no son of mine!"

And John replied out of the fullness of his heart:

"No, thank God, I am not."

The squire turned and looked at him, and the thought came to his mind that, although the young man was living, it was evident that he had lost his mind—the result of marriage with that girl.

John saw that his words had made an impression and said:

"If you will listen, I have a strange story to tell you, but let us forget our differences and go inside of the house. The neighbors are looking and watching our actions."

They entered the house, the squire's curiosity overcoming his anger, and John read the minister's letter to them and produced the birth record. Before he had finished reading the letter, the squire was in a rage. Walking up and down the room and mopping his face with his handkerchief where the perspiration was running down in rivulets, he shouted:

"What tarnal fool yarn is this? Have you gone stark, staring mad? Or are you a drivelling idiot? You are a fool to believe the lies those red devils tell. Did they get any money out of you for it? Of course they did. I never heard of such cussed foolishness."

John waited patiently for the squire to quiet down; then he said:

"The clergyman, whose word is good–"

"Who says he is a clergyman? How do you know his word is good?" broke in the squire.

"–says the story is true, and can be verified by my father and mother, who are anxious to see me."

Ruth commenced to cry, for her mother sat speechless, and the terrified look on her face was pitiful. She seemed incapable of realizing the full import of the story. She told them afterwards "that it seemed for a few minutes as if the foundation of all things was tottering and that her prop was being taken from her."

John tried to comfort her, begging Ruth to calm herself and help him to sustain her mother.

"Yes," sobbed Ruth, "my mother, but not yours. Oh, I cannot believe it."

The squire had started out to find the Indians and demand information of them. When he reached the wigwam he found it deserted. The Indians had decamped after telling their story to John.

After the squire had talked it over with his wife, they agreed that the nurse who had been hired to take care of their little one must be found. Not until she had acknowledged her guilt and verified the Indian story would the squire believe it anything but "a tarnal Injun lie."

It seemed strange and inconsistent of the squire to be so anxious to prove the story untrue. To know that the boy who had been browbeaten and unsympathized with by him all of his young life was not his own son, was a terrible blow to him. He knew and had always known—and been proud of the fact—that John as a boy and man was one out of a hundred, a son that was an honor to his parents and a joy.

But the squire had only one idea—that of keeping his family down and crushed beneath his heel. Then he felt that he was master, and that to his selfish heart and narrow mind was as it should be, proper and right, for a man must rule his own household. He was only one of many who in those days considered it the essence of good government when wife and children trembled beneath the glance of the head of the house, scarcely daring to draw a long breath in his presence without his august permission.

Ruth had never been troubled over her father's disapproval, but John was of a different disposition, timid in his bearing, and through the years of his boyhood had obeyed his father unquestioningly. Ruth often said that she had a mission and that mission was to take some of the nonsense out of her cross old daddy, and she had been the means of making him a little more civilized and decent.

The search for the nurse was of no avail.

John and Sara had determined to go out West. Raguel and Edna sanctioned the journey, and their preparations were speedily effected.

The blind man and his wife eagerly awaited their coming.

Sara had been enjoined by her father not to forget or lose sight of the gall of the fish, so that all should work together for their good and the Indian's prophecy be fulfilled.

When they arrived at their destination the scene was a most affecting one. The mother came to meet them and clasped the hand of her long-lost son. Slowly came the poor blind man; with trembling limbs he walked towards John, guided by the sound of his voice, and in words that were scarcely above a whisper he said:

"It is my son; he has the voice of my father. Oh, that I might look upon his face."

John clasped his arms about him and the two men wept, while Sara tried to sustain and encourage her mother-in-law, saying:

"He is indeed your son. Behold the two faces–they are the counterparts of each other. John is the image of his father. Let us rejoice that the lost is found."

Then, as they rested from their journey, Sara told them the story of her life and brought forth the gall of the fish, saying:

"Father, do not delay the trial of it, for I have faith that your sight will be restored unto you."

And John, whom we shall hereafter designate as Tobias, took the gall and stroked his father's eyes with it, saying:

"Be of good hope, my father."

And Tobit rubbed his eyes because of the smarting, and all of the whiteness that covered them rolled away, and he looked upon his son and embraced him, and then with kindness also welcomed his daughter-in-law, saying:

"You have brought gladness to this house. Abide here with us."

And clasping his wife in his arms, Tobit said:

"Let no evil word ever come between us. Our child has been restored unto us. Together we have suffered, together we share the reward." And with tears mingling with smiles they prayed a prayer of thankfulness, and the sun went down on the re-united family.

With the beginning of the new day the morrow's sunrise brought to them there were many plans for the future. After a few days Tobias and Sara expressed themselves as anxious to return to their home in the East. Tobias's heart clung to the only home that he had ever known, and Sara was homesick for her mother and father. Tobias explained to his father that all of his business interests were there, and he made promise to come back and Visit them twice each year. Then Tobit said to his wife:

"Let us go with the children. There is naught to keep us here. Now that our son is restored let us not lose sight of him, but live where our eyes can rest on him and this dear daughter whom I find is the child of my kinsman, Raguel. The years are not many before we shall be called hence."

So they journeyed to New England, and when they arrived at Kensington, Connecticut, the squire was one of the first to meet them. And when he saw the likeness between the father and son he said:

"God help me, it is true, and I have no dependence for my old age."

No trace of the nurse who had exchanged the dead child for the living one could be found until one year after Sara's wedding day. On that anniversary day the old Indian woman, Silvia Sara, came to see Sara and told her that the nurse's former home had been traced by the Indians. The woman, she said, had gone to the spirit land, but her daughter still lived.

Following the Indian's directions, the woman was found in New Jersey. She told them of her mother's death five years before that date, and of a sealed letter that she had left to her care, with instructions never to open it, but if inquiry was made regarding a dead infant that had once been her charge then she was to produce the letter. The contents would explain everything. The daughter said that she had kept it a sacred trust, although so long a time had elapsed and no inquiry made for it that she had made up her mind that it would never be called for. She was glad to deliver it.

The letter was read, and the story, as they had been told, was confirmed. In small printed letters the woman had set forth all of the facts. She had suffered greatly in her mind, and had often been on the point of confessing the whole thing, but for the fear of being accused of murder and punished by hanging had made her hold her peace. She had been possessed with the idea that no one would believe her story if she said the child's death was accidental, and so for all these years the horror of a death penalty had hovered over her.

Time had set things right so far as justice to the injured could be done. But the years that had gone by, bringing daily sorrow to the stricken parents; could never be undone. The loneliness and uncertainty of those days had left their mark.

Tobias had come into his own again and was glad. To Sara he would always remain John, and Ruth found it difficult to think of him as any one but her dear brother Jack.

Tobit was anxious to have his son go to England and claim the property that had been willed to him by his mother's brother. It was his by every right, and it was his uncle's wish that he should live in the beautiful ancestral home.

When Tobias had been told all of the facts concerning the property and that it had reverted to his old acquaintance, the Lady Sophia Ainslie, because of his supposed death, he refused to make any claim, saying so far as the property was concerned, he had been virtually dead all these years, and it should remain the Lady Sophia's home. He relinquished all claim and had all legalities attended to, so there could be nothing to prevent the Lady Sophia from holding the property.

There had been great consternation at the castle when the news came that her aunt's son had been found. She had grown to look upon the old place as her own, resting securely in the belief that after all these years there was little likelihood of his being alive, and that her claim would never be disputed.

She listened to the strange story of his life and restoration to his parents in consternation, and when told that her cousin was the young man known as the squire's son she was greatly chagrined and said to her Aunt Charlotte, who was deeply lamenting the fact that they would in all probability have to vacate their beautiful home:

"If I had known I might have married him. Then all would have been secured to me."

That was like the Lady Sophia, to ignore the truth that John had never given her any reason to suppose that he would care for such an alliance. Her aunt smiled, but was too wise to contradict her. The situation seemed serious, for it never entered the heads of these scheming women that any man in his right senses would voluntarily give up such a property.

Tobias was a good American and had no desire to leave his own country, and he considered that morally he had no right to the property left to him with the expectation that he would marry the Lady Sophia and keep the estate intact. He knew that nothing would have tempted him to carry out any such designs.

His generosity was appreciated, judging from what the Lady Sophia said, "that when she 'eard hit she could scarcely believe 'er hears. Hand hit was strange what fools those Americans were."

Tobias and Sara prospered and were exceedingly happy.

The old squire never recovered from the blow. When it was proven to his satisfaction that John was not his son he broke down and wept.

The Indian woman pointed out the spot in the woods where his little son was buried by the Indians. The squire bought the land and erected a stone to mark the place. It was placed flat above the ground in the form of a table, and had inscribed thereon the facts concerning the little one's death.

The squire's mind gradually failed until from a stern, unbending, arbitrary man he became gentle and childlike in his demeanor. He spent many hours in the woods by the side of the little grave, always depending on Ruth for companionship, and was docile and happy when she was with him.

Her mother was the first to go away from them. After a long illness that was a gradual wasting away, she departed this life. She clung to John as long as she lived, and he was the same good son to her unto the last. She died with her hand clasped in his—her last words, "My son,"—he answered, "Yes, Mother." A peaceful smile rested on the tired face.

His own mother knew that she could never expect to hold the same place in his heart that had been given to the dead woman, whom he had always known as mother, and to whom he had given his child-heart. She had guided his footsteps from childhood to manhood with wise and faithful counsel, and it was natural and right that he should look up to her and cherish the only mother-love that he had ever known.

Nor would his own mother have it any different. Yet sometimes the mother-heart in her breast cried out until she felt that the strain was almost unendurable. The knowledge that she had been deprived of her rights—the happiness of training the child-mind and lavishing the mother-love that all these wasted years had been pent up and re strained while the child had been away from his rightful home—was hard to bear.

Tobias gave to her a gentle deference and respect, and in all ways was a good, dutiful son, and she realized that she owed much to the gentle woman who had filled her place to him. He was a son to be proud of, intelligent, kind and helpful to his fellowmen, an ideal husband and father—for a tiny girl had come to bless the home of Tobias and Sara. The baby had blue eyes like her mother, and displayed her father's sturdy ways. She was named Ruth Edna. Ruth would have it so, and from the hour of her birth had called her Ruth II.

Ruth had never wavered in her sisterly allegiance to Sara from the day that her brother "Jack" had asked her to look upon her as a sister. Ruth, like her namesake of old, was of loyal nature.

Abby Ann was a devoted worshiper of the baby, and she was at work every spare moment on patch work quilts and preparing linen against the time when little Ruth should need a dowry, for she must have as good "a setting out" as her mother had had before her.

Sara was a grand woman; after much sorrow and tribulation her feet had entered the path of peace her character had become strengthened by her trials and her disposition sweetened by adversity. Where a weaker character would have succumbed she had risen above her troubles, and looked down in calm wonder at the narrow minds that had been so ready to accuse and believe in her guilt when she was guiltless—the crimes existing only in the minds that were incapable of taking a broader view of life and giving the accused, where there was no proof of wrong, the benefit of the doubt. When Sara reviewed her past life, the strange events and peculiar history of her early years, she knew that until John became her lover-husband and the father of her children she had never known the true, abiding love that now filled to overflowing the measure of her happiness.

When Ruth was two years old a little boy was born. His grandma Anna asked the privilege of naming him Tobias, and teaching and caring for his welfare filled her declining years with joy, and she began her mother-life again, going back in thought and spirit to that period when her little son was stolen from her. The baby features were like what his father's were in infancy, and it seemed to her that God had sent him to gladden her heart and make amends to her for all the sad years that she had been bereft.

Sara's children were wisely trained, and many of the bright men and women that New England has sent out in the world to achieve fame and renown are proud to claim her as the source of an unblemished lineage.

One after the other the old family has been called away from earth, and their earthly forms have been laid away to rest in the quiet burying ground in Kensington.

The Indians and their wigwams are seen in those parts no more, but the rugged path through Cat Hole Pass is the same as in "ye olden tyme" when Sara's life drama was enacted.

In the spring and summer, aye, many times in winter, the birds sing and hold carnival as in the days of yore. The beautiful blossoms of the dogwood trees in the month of May droop in creamy splendor and the scent of the honeysuckle is in the air. A tangled wilderness of vines and flowers in wood and dell meet the delighted eyes of those who wander over the old ground, where violets purple and white nod their sweet heads by the side of the beautiful Quinnipiac River, the silver glint of its waters mirroring the surrounding beauties of trees and landscape. And the sun goes down each night in splendor beyond the glories of hanging hills and wooded dells, where grand old West Peak, towering and majestic, stands guard above them all.